"There are still th
Swimming in the
little smile contin
Marietta's mouth. "Naked.

And just like that, the steady, persistent hum of awareness in Nico's blood intensified—until he felt as if a high-voltage current were arcing through his veins.

"Somewhere private, of course," she said. "Your beach would be perfect!"

An image of Marietta naked in the clear water at the foot of his cliff flashed into his head. Heat and lust ignited in his belly—along with a stab of anger.

She *did* feel the pull of attraction, the crackle of awareness in the air between them. He could see it—the sudden hectic color in her cheeks, the way her eyes glittered and held his in silent challenge.

She was provoking him.

Playing with fire.

He lunged up out of his chair, strode to her side and seized her chin. The dark, angry look he gave her should have intimidated. Instead her lips parted, soft and inviting, as though she were anticipating...a *kiss*.

Dieu.

He wanted to kiss her. Wanted to crush his mouth onto hers and let her feel the full unleashed power of the lust she was deliberately inciting. Wanted to *punish* her for dangling temptation in front of him like a treat he didn't deserve.

He held himself rigid. Controlled.

"Be *very* careful what you wish for, Marietta."

And then he released her and stalked into the house, back to the relative safety of his study—where he should have had the sense to stay in the first place.

Irresistible Mediterranean Tycoons

Impossibly arrogant, overwhelmingly sexy...
Meet the men you can't say no to!

Gorgeous, powerful and darkly brooding,
Leo Vincenti and Nicolas César have dominated
their fields not only in their home countries
of Italy and France but across the globe.

Now it's time for them to turn their unwavering
focus to a different challenge—conquering two
defiantly delectable heroines of their own!

But have these billionaires bitten off more
than they can chew?

Find out in:

Surrendering to the Vengeful Italian

Defying Her Billionaire Protector

Available now!

Angela Bissell

——

DEFYING HER BILLIONAIRE PROTECTOR

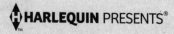

HARLEQUIN PRESENTS®

Recycling programs
for this product may
not exist in your area.

ISBN-13: 978-0-373-06036-8

Defying Her Billionaire Protector

First North American Publication 2016

Copyright © 2016 by Angela Bissell

www.Harlequin.com

Printed in U.S.A.

Angela Bissell lives with her husband and one crazy Ragdoll cat in the vibrant harborside city of Wellington, New Zealand. In her twenties, with a wad of savings and a few meager possessions, she took off for Europe, backpacking through Egypt, Israel, Turkey and the Greek islands before finding her way to London, where she settled and worked in a glamorous hotel for several years. Clearly the perfect grounding for her love of Harlequin Presents! Visit her at angelabissell.com.

Books by Angela Bissell

Harlequin Presents

Irresistible Mediterranean Tycoons
Surrendering to the Vengeful Italian

Visit Harlequin.com for more titles.

For my friend Lisa, a brave, beautiful and inspiring woman. Thank you for your valuable insights— and for letting me have a spin in your wheels. Here's to many more Princess Days in the sun!

CHAPTER ONE

'*MAMMA MIA!* HERE they come.'

Marietta's hands stilled over the keys of her computer, her assistant's warning—low-voiced yet laced with an unmistakable thread of anticipation—shattering her train of thought like crystal under a hammer. She looked up in time to see the courier pushing open the glass doors of the gallery she managed in the heart of Rome's affluent Parioli district. In his arms he cradled a huge, hand-tied bouquet of roses.

'*Bellissimo.*' Lina moved from the storeroom doorway and stood by Marietta's desk at the rear of the gallery. 'They are the best yet!'

Marietta would have liked to disagree with that assessment, but Lina was right. The long-stemmed roses *were* beautiful, each head—at least two dozen of them—exquisite, the velvety petals a vivid red that in the whiteness of the gallery made Marietta think, perversely, of blood.

Her thoughts snapped to the elegant spray of white

orchids that had been delivered earlier in the week—
surprisingly, because until then the flowers had always arrived on a Friday. Pretty and delicate, the
orchids, like the roses, had been lovely to look at,
but their sweet, cloying scent had lingered in her
nostrils and left her feeling faintly ill long after she
had disposed of them.

Even the note that had come with them had been
heavily perfumed, and she'd wanted to destroy that
too. Had wanted to rip the card and its intimate typewritten message into tiny, indecipherable pieces and
flush them down the toilet.

But she'd been told to keep the notes in case they
held any clues, so she'd shoved the card into a drawer,
along with all the others, and vowed that when this
was over—when her secret-admirer-turned-stalker
was caught or simply grew tired of his antics—she
would set a match to those cards and enjoy watching them burn.

The courier strode over the polished concrete towards them, and Marietta felt her stomach doing
a little surge and roll. She didn't want to touch the
roses. She definitely didn't want them near enough
for her to smell.

'Ciao.'

The young courier's broad smile did nothing to
quell her dread. His gaze shifted sideways—drawn,
unsurprisingly, to Lina's tall, willowy form—and
Marietta saw the predictable flare of male appre-

ciation on his face give way to surprise—or maybe
shock was a better word—the moment the man sitting behind her stood.

He strode around her desk, straight into the courier's path, and she imagined she heard the young
man's jaw crack, his mouth dropped open so fast.
His face lost its colour, paling several shades as he
took in the large, imposing man before him. She felt
a twinge of sympathy for the guy; Nicolas César,
ex-legionnaire, head of the widely revered global
conglomerate César Security and her brother's good
friend, could scare the wits out of most people—
and that was on the days he *didn't* look hell-bent on
throttling someone.

He stared down at the courier from his massive
height and extended a large, capable-looking hand.
A hand that appeared elegant and bone-crushingly
strong all at the same time. 'Give them to me.'

Nico's deep voice rumbled with the kind of natural authority only a fool with no thought for self-
preservation would dare to challenge. Wisely, the
younger man didn't hesitate. He handed over the
roses with a haste that might have amused Marietta had anything about this situation been remotely
funny. His eyes darted back to Lina, but her attention was firmly fixed on the other man, and, as if
understanding he couldn't possibly compete with all
that eye-popping masculinity, the courier shot Marietta a bemused look and hurried out of the gallery.

She gripped the titanium hand rims on the wheels of her custom-made chair and reversed a few feet from her desk. Although Nico stood on the other side, with a great slab of horizontal glass between them, she needed the comfort of the extra distance before she looked at him.

Not, she told herself, because she wasn't used to looking up at people. Thirteen years in a wheelchair had accustomed her to seeing the world from a diminished height, and she'd long ago reconciled herself to that aspect of her disability. And although able-bodied people often thought of her as being *confined* to a wheelchair—as though the chair and not her paralysed legs were the prison—for Marietta the use of her modern, ultralight chair for mobility was a choice. One that gave her the freedom to work and travel. To live her life with a level of independence any single, career-focused woman of thirty would wish to enjoy.

But Nicolas César wasn't anything like the people Marietta encountered on an ordinary day, and it wasn't only his unique physicality that set him apart—wasn't only the impressive breadth of his shoulders, the fact that he stood taller than most. On par with her six-foot-four brother—or the fact that his dark trousers and close-fitting black shirt moulded the kind of lean, hard-muscled physique that spoke of discipline and sweat and the good fortune of strong, resilient genes. Rather, it was the raw power he exuded from every inch of that undeniably masculine frame—the overriding impression that here was a man few others dared trifle with—that made Marietta's hormones sit up and take notice.

Which irritated her enormously.

Sexual attraction was a complication she didn't need in her life right now—or *ever*, for that matter. Especially to a man so far out of her physical league her pride smarted just to look at him.

'Are you not going to interrogate him?' she asked, and her annoyance with herself—with that hot, inescapable lick of feminine awareness—lent her words a much pithier edge than she'd intended.

Dark blue eyes thinned and settled on her, making her aware that her sarcasm wasn't lost on Nico, and guilt instantly pricked her. He was here to help because her brother had asked him to. That Leo had done so without consulting her first was no fault of Nico's. Unleashing her frustration on him was childish. Unfair.

He held her gaze, his silent, prolonged eye contact causing her skin to flush and her insides to squirm with something far more unsettling than guilt. She didn't look away and wasn't sure she could even if she wanted to. His eyes were such a dark, mesmerising blue. Staring into them made her feel as if she'd been dragged beneath the surface of a vast, bottomless sea and could no longer breathe.

She opened her mouth to offer an apology—and

drag some much-needed air into her lungs—but Nico spoke first.

'Bruno has cleared the staff at the florist's shop and vetted the couriers they use. There is no need for me to...' he paused for a fraction of a beat '...*interrogate* him.'

That slight yet deliberate emphasis on the word *interrogate* elevated Marietta's discomfort. Looking at him, it wasn't at all difficult for her to visualise Nicolas César in the role of interrogator—nor did she have any trouble imagining that anyone on the wrong side of that arrangement would quickly find themselves either pleading for mercy or spilling their deepest, darkest secrets to him. Or both.

At the same time, she imagined any man who possessed that degree of dark, potent magnetism would rarely, if ever, want for female companionship. Women flocked to him wherever he went, no doubt, drawn like hummingbirds to nectar by his hard-edged looks and his big, powerful body.

And that would be *before* he opened his mouth.

Before that deep-timbre voice, with its French accent and slight North American inflection, poured over them like heated syrup and turned their insides all gooey.

Marietta suppressed a little shiver.

Did Nico make his lovers plead?

Did he make them scream?

The shiver turned into a hot flush that cascaded

through Marietta's body and scalded her from the inside out. *Madre di Dio.* What was wrong with her? She had no business allowing her thoughts to veer in that direction. No business entertaining hot, lurid fantasies about her brother's friend. Life had taught her some harsh lessons—lessons that had moulded her into a realist—and realists like her did not waste their time fantasising about things they would never have.

And yet she wasn't without aspirations. Cementing her place in the art world, achieving success and recognition as an artist in her own right, supporting herself independently of her brother's wealth and generosity—*those* were her goals, the dreams that got her out of bed in the mornings.

Plus she had a wish list tucked away—a 'bucket list', some people called it. Everyone had one, didn't they? Everyone wanted to see things and do things that breathed some excitement, some *magic* into their ordinary lives.

Marietta was no different. As an incomplete paraplegic she could no longer walk, but living with a spinal cord injury didn't mean she couldn't push her own boundaries, do things that were a little adventurous or wild.

Paraplegics around the world skydived and flew planes and competed in rigorous sports.

Every item on Marietta's wish list was doable. Some more challenging than others, given her physical limitations, but all of them realistic. She certainly didn't have her head in the clouds. She knew what was possible and what wasn't. And there was no reason whatsoever that she couldn't tandem skydive. Or float in a hot air balloon. Or travel to Egypt to see the pyramids.

But what were the chances of a man who could crook his finger and have any woman in the world—any *able-bodied* woman in the world—he wanted desiring her?

Now *that* was pure fantasy—a pointless, fanciful daydream she needn't waste her time indulging.

What she did need to do was stay focused, remember what was important: her job, her independence, her art.

Especially her art.

But now all of that was under threat. In danger of being disrupted by some anonymous admirer who *must* be mentally unstable, or, if she were being less kind, completely deranged.

Six weeks. That was how long she'd been receiving the bunches of flowers and the notes she'd thought quaint and amusing—even flattering—at first. But over the weeks the messages had gone from sweet to intense, their content growing more personal, more intimate. More possessive.

It was the note that had come with a bouquet of thirteen crimson tulips on a Friday two weeks ago, however, that had for the first time left her truly spooked.

Such a beautiful dress you wore yesterday, amore mio. *Red is perfect on you—and my favourite colour. You see? We were made for each other! S.*

Those words had clamped a cold fist around her throat and squeezed hard as their import had slowly sunk in. And she had realised something she hadn't considered before then—that he, whoever *he* was, was following her, watching her, *stalking* her.

Gooseflesh rose on Marietta's forearms and she resisted the urge to rub them, to scrub away the sensation of something unpleasant crawling over her skin.

She'd been so shaken she'd confided in her sister-in-law, Helena—which in hindsight had been a mistake. Helena, in spite of Marietta's pleas for her not to, had told her husband—Marietta's brother—who had, of course, flipped. Within minutes Leo had been on the phone, severely chastising her for not going directly to him and urging her to involve the police.

Advice she'd promptly ignored. She hadn't wanted to create a fuss and her big brother was, as always, being over-protective. The fact he'd waited an entire forty-eight hours before calling on his friend Nico for assistance was, she reflected now, nothing short of astonishing.

That Nico, whom she'd last seen at Leo and Helena's wedding two years before, had, in the first instance, sent his man Bruno rather than handle the matter himself, was something Marietta had *not*, she'd assured herself, been a little disappointed about.

Nicolas César was, after all, a busy man—CEO of a renowned global network that provided security and protection services to some of the world's most powerful corporations and influential figureheads. Dealing with an overzealous admirer was never going to figure high on his priority list, no matter how solid his friendship with her brother.

And yet…here he stood. Or perhaps *towered* was the better word, she thought, conscious of a crick in her neck. Of the warm pulse of blood beneath her skin. Her heartbeat had not quite settled back into its normal rhythm since he'd walked, unannounced, into the gallery some forty minutes earlier.

After a brief, polite greeting he'd asked to see the cards Bruno had told her to keep, and then, despite the fact they were written in Italian, had proceeded to read every intimate word until Marietta's face had burned with mortified heat. Then—since it was mid-afternoon on a Friday, and that meant another bouquet was likely on its way—he'd commandeered one of the soft chairs reserved for the gallery's clientele and artists and waited for the flowers she had silently prayed wouldn't come.

'Where's Bruno?' she asked now. Not because she missed the rigid presence of the dark-suited man, but rather because she could see the small white envelope attached to the roses and wanted to delay, if only for a minute longer, having to open it.

'Following up a lead.'

A lead. That sounded vague. 'What sort of lead?'

He didn't answer her. Instead he turned to Lina, as if he'd not heard the question or had simply chosen to ignore it.

Marietta tamped down her annoyance—only to feel it flare again when she glanced at her assistant. *Santo cielo!* Had the girl no pride? No sense of dignity? Marietta wanted to snap her fingers at her. Tell her to wipe that silly doe-eyed look off her face. To straighten up and pull her hip back in, instead of jutting it sideways in a come-hither pose she probably wasn't even aware she'd adopted.

Nico detached the envelope from the roses, his strong fingers snapping the straw ribbon like a strand of cotton, and handed the bouquet to Lina. 'Get rid of them.'

Lina—foolish girl—beamed at him as if he'd paid her a compliment rather than barked an order at her. Marietta bristled on her assistant's behalf. Lina, however, was oblivious. Without so much as glancing at Marietta for confirmation, she took the roses and disappeared out to the back—heading, presumably, for the outdoor dumpster behind the building.

Marietta couldn't help herself. 'That was rude.'

Nico's eyes narrowed on her again…so blue. So disconcerting. 'Pardon?'

'Lina,' she clarified. 'You could have asked nicely. Barking commands at people is rude.'

One heavy eyebrow arced, ever so slightly, towards his dark brown hairline. 'She did not look upset.'

Of course she hadn't looked upset. She'd looked smitten and flushed and…*ravenous*. As if she'd wanted to drag Nico into the storeroom, bolt the door shut and tear his clothes off—with her teeth.

Marietta was sure Nico knew it, too.

And yet, to his credit, he hadn't encouraged her attentions. Hadn't seemed to give out any inappropriate cues. In fact he'd seemed barely to notice her— unlike some of the male visitors to the gallery, who appeared more entranced by Lina's legs than by the sculptures and paintings on display.

And the girl had good legs—long and shapely— and a good body that she dressed, or on occasion *under*dressed, to showcase. Why shouldn't she? She was tall and graceful. Feminine, yet lithe.

Unbroken.

Everything Marietta might have been and wasn't, thanks to one fateful split-second decision. One irreversible moment of teenage stupidity. A moment that had altered the course of her life and shattered what little had remained of her childhood innocence.

Still—as a few well-intentioned if slightly insensitive people had pointed out during the long, excruciating months of her rehabilitation—she'd been lucky.

She had survived.

The three teens in the car with her—including the alcohol-impaired driver—had not. Two had died on impact with the concrete median barrier, the third on a gurney surrounded by the trauma team trying desperately to save her.

For Marietta, the sole survivor of that tragic car crash, a long string of dark, torturous days had followed. Days when she'd lain unable or sometimes unwilling to move, staring at the ceiling of the hated rehab unit. Reliving those final moments with her friends and wishing, in her darkest moments, that she had died alongside them.

But she had not died.

She had fought her way back.

For the brother whom she knew had taken the burden of responsibility—and blame—upon himself. For the second chance at life she'd been given that her friends had not. For her mother—God rest her soul—who would have wanted Marietta to fight with the same courage and determination with which she'd battled the cancer that had, in the end, cruelly won. And—even though she'd stayed angry with him for a long time after he'd died—for her father, who'd fought his own grief-fuelled demons after his wife's death and tragically lost.

Her chin went up a notch.

She had faced down every brutal obstacle the universe had thrown at her and she was still here. She would *not* let some stranger, some clearly unhinged individual, disrupt the life she'd worked so long and hard to rebuild. And she certainly wasn't afraid of some pathetic words on a little white card.

She held out her hand for the envelope. Nico hesitated, then handed it over. Willing her hands not to shake, she tore open the flap and pulled out the card. She sucked in a deep breath and started to read—and felt the cold pasta salad she'd had for lunch threaten to vacate her stomach.

Marietta's hands had started to shake.

She glanced up, her espresso-coloured eyes so dark Nico couldn't differentiate between iris and pupil. They were glassy, enormous—larger than usual—and, he noted, unblinking. Combined with her sudden pallor, the tremor in her slim hands, they conveyed an emotion Nico had more than once in his life been intimately acquainted with.

Fear.

He cursed under his breath, reached over the glass-topped desk and whipped the card out of her hands.

His Italian wasn't impeccable, like his native

French or his English, but he had no trouble reading the typewritten words. His fingers tightened on the card but he took care to keep his face expressionless. Marietta was a strong woman—something he'd intuited the first time they'd met in passing at her brother's office, and again at Leo's wedding—but right now she was shaken and he needed her to be calm. Reassured. *Safe.*

Anything less would be a disservice to her brother, and Leo was a good friend—had been ever since their paths had crossed via a mutual client eight years ago. Nico had recognised in the Italian the qualities of a man he could like and respect. Leo's company specialised in cyber security, and his people occasionally lent their technical expertise to Nico's own. Outside of business the two men had become firm friends—and Nico did not intend to let his friend down.

He slipped the card into a plastic folder along with the others. Aside from an insight into their composer's mind, the notes offered nothing of real value and no means by which they could track the original sender. The flowers were always ordered online, the cards printed by the florist, the words simply copied from the order's electronic message field.

Bruno had been confident at first. Online orders meant a traceable digital trail to IP addresses and credit cards. But whoever Marietta's stalker was he was careful—and clever. Their tech guys had chased their tails through a series of redirected addresses and discovered the account with the florist had been opened using bogus details. The invoices were sent to a rented mailbox and payments were received in cash via mail.

It all indicated a level of premeditation and intent neither Nico nor Bruno had anticipated. And Nico didn't like it. Didn't like it that he'd underestimated the threat—assuming, at first, that they'd be dealing with nothing more troublesome than a jilted boyfriend. It galled him now to accept that he'd been wrong because he knew better than to assume.

But he was here now, in Rome, with the meetings he'd had scheduled for today in New York cancelled after Bruno's call twenty-four hours earlier.

And they *would* find this guy. They'd break some rules, sidestep some local bureaucracy, and they would find him.

He strode around the desk and dropped to his haunches in front of Marietta's chair, bringing his eyes level with hers. She jerked back a little, as if she wasn't used to such an action, and he wondered briefly if it were not the accepted thing to do. But he'd have done the same with any woman he sought to reassure, conscious that his height, his sheer size, might intimidate.

'We *will* stop him, Marietta.'

Her eyes remained huge in her face, her olive

complexion stripped of colour. 'He's been in my home…'

Nico ground his jaw. 'Perhaps.'

'But the note—'

'Could be nothing more than a scare tactic,' he cut in. Yet the tension in his gut, the premonitory prickle at his nape, told him the truth was something far less palatable. More sinister.

I have left you a gift, tesoro. *On your bed. Think of me when you unwrap it. Sleep well,* amore mio. *S.*

On impulse he took her hand—small compared to his, and yet strong rather than dainty or delicate. Her fingers were slender and long, her nails short and neat, manicured at home, he guessed, rather than by a professional.

Incredibly, Nico could still remember clasping her hand on their very first introduction—four, maybe five years ago at her brother's office. Their handshake had been brief but he'd noted that her skin felt cool, pleasant to the touch, her palm soft and smooth in places, callused in others. He remembered, too, seeing her at Leo's wedding a couple of years later. Remembered watching her, intrigued and impressed with the way she handled her wheelchair—as if it were a natural extension of her body.

In the church she'd glided down the aisle before the bride, composed and confident, unselfconscious—or at least that was the impression she'd given. Her sister-in-law, a beautiful English woman, had looked stunning in a simple white gown, but it was Marietta to whom Nico's attention had been repeatedly drawn throughout the ceremony.

In his thirty-six years he'd attended two other weddings—his own, which he preferred not to dwell upon, and an equally lavish affair in the Bahamas to which he had, regrettably, allowed a former lover to drag him—but he could not recall a bridesmaid at either who might have outshone Marietta in looks or elegance.

With her thick mahogany hair piled high on her head, the golden skin of her shoulders and décolletage bare above the turquoise silk of her long bridesmaid's sheath, the fact she was in a wheelchair had not diminished the impact of her beauty.

And then there were the shoes.

Nico could not forget the shoes.

Stilettos.

Sexy, feminine, four-inch stilettos in a bright turquoise to match the gown.

That Marietta could not walk in those shoes had made him admire her all the more for wearing them. It was a statement—a bold one—as though she were flipping the bird to her disability...or rather to anyone who thought a woman who couldn't walk was wasting her time wearing sexy shoes, and it had made him want to smile.

Hell, it had made him want to grin.

And that was an urge he rarely experienced.

'Nico?'

Marietta's hand twitched in his, jerking his thoughts back to the present. He refocused, realised his thumb was stroking small circles over her skin. Abruptly he broke contact and stood. 'Stay here. Keep Lina with you.'

She wheeled back and looked up at him. 'Where are you going?'

'Your apartment.'

She frowned, a smudge of colour returning to her face. 'Not without me, you're not.'

'It is better that you stay here,' he said evenly.

'Why?'

When he hesitated a fraction too long, her fine-boned features twisted into a look of horror.

'*Mio Dio*. You think he might be there, don't you?' She stared at him accusingly. 'But you said the note was just a scare tactic.'

'*Could* be,' he corrected. 'I won't know for certain until I've checked it out.'

'Then I'll come with you.'

'I'd prefer you didn't.'

Her shoulders snapped back, her eyes, wide with shock and fear only seconds before, now narrowing. 'It's my apartment. I'm coming whether you *prefer* it or not.' Her delicate chin lifted. 'Besides, you need me. You won't get in without my security code and key.'

'Both of which you are about to give to me,' he told her, keeping his voice reasonable even as he felt his patience slipping. He was unaccustomed to people arguing with him—especially women.

Marietta folded her hands in her lap. The gesture combined with her conservative attire—a sleeveless high-necked lilac silk blouse, long black pants and, perhaps less conservative, a pair of purple high-heeled suede boots—made her look almost demure. Yet there was nothing demure in the set of her shoulders or the bright glint of defiance in her eyes.

'Do people always jump when you bark?'

He crossed his arms over his chest. Outwardly he was calm. Inside, impatience heated his blood dangerously close to tipping point. *'Oui,'* he said, injecting a low note of warning into his voice he hoped she had the wisdom to heed. 'If they know what is good for them.'

Her eyebrows rose at that, but the shrug that rolled off her shoulders was careless. 'Well, I'm sorry to disappoint you—' she looked pointedly at her legs and then back at him '—but you might have noticed I can't jump very high these days.'

Nico flattened his mouth, returned her stare. Channelled his trademark control—or tried to. 'You are wasting time, Marietta.'

'Me?' Somehow she managed to look utterly innocent. 'You're the one holding us up, Nico. We could have been halfway there by now.'

He sucked in a breath and exhaled sharply. Leo had warned him that Marietta could be stubborn. Resolute. Headstrong. No doubt those qualities had served her well through some difficult times, helped her overcome the kind of obstacles most people, if they were fortunate, would never have to face in their lifetime. He respected those qualities, admired them, but right now he'd settle for a lot less lip and a great deal more acquiescence.

The determined glitter in those liquid brown eyes told him he had zero chance of getting it. Nico couldn't decide if that surprised him, impressed him, or angered him.

People did not defy Nicolas César.

They *obeyed* him.

Fortunately for Marietta he had neither the time nor the patience to stand there and argue. He uncrossed his arms. Muttered an oath. 'Wait here,' he growled. 'I'll bring my car to the front of the gallery and collect you.'

A smile broke on her face that almost made the pain of his capitulation worth it. He blinked. *Mon Dieu.* Did she give that smile freely to everyone she met? If so, he wouldn't be surprised to find a thousand infatuated admirers lurking in the wings.

'No need,' she said, and rolled her chair forward

to a small cabinet beside her desk. She pulled out an enormous leather handbag. 'I have my car in the lane out back. I'll drive myself and meet you there.'

Lina reappeared at that moment, minus the roses. She tossed her blonde hair over one too bony shoulder and gave him a smile that lacked even a fraction of the impact of Marietta's.

'Can you please close up tonight, Lina?' Marietta said to the girl. 'I doubt I'll be back. Call me if you need anything. I'll see you in the morning.' She lifted her gaze to Nico's. 'I suppose you already know my address?'

'Oui,' he said, and noted with a small punch of satisfaction how her pretty mouth tightened at that.

'Okay. Well, I'll see you there, then.' She wheeled past him, towards the rear of the gallery.

'Marietta.'

She stopped, glanced over her shoulder at him. *'Si?'*

'If you get there first, wait for me. Do not go in.'

Her mouth pursed. 'Is that an order?'

'You may consider it one.'

Only the flare of her fine nostrils betrayed her annoyance. 'Very well,' she said, then continued on her way.

For a moment Nico watched her go, her long dark hair swinging behind her, her olive-skinned arms, defined by muscle yet still slender and feminine, propelling the wheels of her chair forward with strong, confident movements.

She disappeared through a rear door and Nico spun away, making his own exit through the front of the gallery and down a short flight of stone steps. He strode along the wide tree-lined street to where he'd parked the silver sports car Bruno had had waiting at the airport for him this morning when his jet had landed.

He wrenched open the driver's door and scowled.

He would very much enjoy giving Marietta a lesson in obedience, but he had no doubt her brother would kill him—slowly and painfully—if he knew the methods Nico had in mind.

CHAPTER TWO

MARIETTA DROVE HER bright yellow sedan into the basement of her apartment building and swung into her reserved space near the elevator. She cut the engine, pushed the door open and used her arms to shift herself around until her legs dangled out of the car.

She loved her modified car. In addition to its customised hand controls, the rear passenger door on the driver's side had been altered to open in the reverse direction, so she could reach around from the driver's seat, open the door and pull her wheelchair out of the back. She did so now, and with a little shuffling, some careful hand placements and a couple of well-executed manoeuvres she transferred herself out of the car and into her chair.

It was a routine refined and perfected through years of practice, and one she could probably perform in her sleep.

She put her handbag in her lap and took the elevator to the lobby, confident Nico couldn't have beaten her there despite the extra minutes she'd needed to get in and out of her car. He probably had a faster, flashier set of wheels, but she knew the roads between here and the gallery like the back of her hand—not to mention half a dozen shortcuts only a local would know to use.

And yet when she rolled out of the elevator onto the lobby's shiny sand-coloured marble, there he stood. She frowned, confused as much as miffed. The building, she knew, was secure, the double doors from the street controlled by keypad access day and night. 'How did you get inside?'

'One of your neighbours was on his way out and let me in.' His voice was dark. His expression, too. *'Imbécile.'*

His deep scowl deterred her from jumping to the defence of whichever neighbour had earned his disapproval. The man had no doubt thought nothing of it, but even Marietta had to admit that giving entry to a stranger off the street showed a dreadful disregard for security.

'I'm on the ground floor,' she said, deciding to leave that subject well enough alone, and wheeled her chair around.

Silent, his big body radiating tension like ripples of heat from a furnace, Nico followed her through the lobby, across the quiet interior courtyard with its great pots of manicured topiaries and into a small vestibule housing the front doors of her apartment and one other. As soon as they stopped his hand appeared, palm up, in front of her face.

'Key.'

For a second—just a second—Marietta contemplated ignoring his curt command, but this, she acknowledged, was not the time for bravado. Her stalker might have been in her home.

Her stalker might *still* be in her home.

Her stomach gave a sharp, sickening twist and she promptly handed over the key and watched, heart thumping, as Nico unlocked the door.

'Stay here,' he ordered, and she nodded, her mouth suddenly far too dry to protest. He went in, leaving the door an inch ajar behind him.

Marietta clutched her handbag in her lap and waited. Endless minutes ticked by, followed by more endless minutes. When Nico still hadn't reappeared and she could no longer stand the suspense, she nudged the door open, inched forward and hovered on the threshold.

'Nico?' she called out, her voice echoing off the parquet wood flooring in the entry hall.

Nothing.

'Nico!' she tried again, louder this time.

Still nothing.

This was ridiculous. She wheeled down the hallway, a hot mix of impatience and adrenaline spurring her on.

'I told you to stay put.'

Nico's deep voice slammed into her from behind. She turned her chair around and blinked, her brain instantly grappling to interpret what her eyes were seeing. The sight of Nico standing in her bedroom doorway—which, in her haste, she'd sailed straight by—was easy enough to compute. The rest—the blue latex gloves sheathing his large hands, something red and lacy dangling from his fingers—was enough to send her senses into a floor-tilting spin.

She stared at the bizarre image before her a moment longer, until her breathing resumed some kind of normal rhythm, then gripped the hand rims of her chair and started forward—only to have Nico plant his feet firmly in the doorway and block her path.

She hiked up her chin, wishing there was a way to plough through that imposing wall of muscle. 'Let me in,' she demanded, and reached for the scrap of red lace.

He jerked it out of reach. 'Marietta—'

'No. This is *my* home, Nico. Whatever he's done, whatever he's left for me, I want to see.'

It took every shred of determination she possessed not to back down under the full force of Nico's reprimanding stare. Finally, just as she began to think he wouldn't budge, his rigid stance loosened.

He pointed a latex-clad finger at her. 'Do not touch anything. There could be DNA and prints to lift.' Then he stepped aside, allowing her to enter.

Marietta's gaze went straight to the bed. To the

crimson box lying open on her cream cotton coverlet and the items of luxury lingerie spilling haphazardly from between layers of soft white tissue. Scattered around the box and all across her bed were dozens upon dozens of red and white rose petals.

She moved closer, made out a red satin and black lace chemise, a sheer negligee and a pair of skimpy scarlet knickers. She closed her eyes, turned away, fighting a sudden stab of nausea. When she opened them again, her gaze landed on the item in Nico's hand. A bra, she registered now. A lacy, see-through concoction designed to be sexy and revealing as opposed to any kind of practical.

Her gaze jerked up, collided with Nico's, and for a fleeting moment it seemed as though something arced in the air between them. Something hot and bright and electric.

Which just went to prove how easily stress could affect the mind—because surely she had imagined that strange ripple of energy in the room that had felt almost like… What? Sexual awareness?

Heat flooded her face. *Si*, she was definitely stressed—not to mention embarrassed and *horrified*.

She yanked her gaze away from Nico's and took one last look at her bed. Did her stalker think he would one day share it with her? Thick bile coated her throat and the heat drained from her face, leaving her cold and clammy.

'Was there a card?' she managed to ask.

Nico turned away from her to lay the bra on the bed. 'No,' he said, snapping the gloves off his hands. He turned back to look at her, his blue eyes dark and unreadable. 'You're pale, Marietta. Do you have anything to drink?'

She nodded. *Si*, a drink…something to wash the bile out of her throat, shave the edge off her nerves. She wheeled out of the room. She wouldn't be able to sleep here tonight. Perhaps she could stay at Leo's penthouse for the weekend? He'd be travelling to Tuscany this evening, back to Helena and their adorable baby boy Riccardo. Leo's apartment building—a stunning renovated historic structure in the heart of the old city—wasn't as wheelchair-friendly as this one, but there was an elevator at least. Or perhaps she could telephone a girlfriend?

Her mind spun in jerky circles until she reached her lounge and paused. She looked around the cosy, light-filled room. Had her stalker been in here, too? Had he snooped through every inch of her beloved home? Had he *touched* her things?

Angry and sickened, she dumped her handbag on her plum-coloured sofa and headed for the solid oak sideboard. The cabinet housed a small selection of spirits—brandy, *limoncello*, and a bottle of whisky for her brother when he visited.

She grabbed two cut-glass tumblers and, hearing footsteps on the hardwood floor behind her, twisted her chin round to look at Nico. 'What will you have?'

He shrugged, the movement accentuating the breadth of his shoulders under his black open-necked shirt. 'Whatever you're having.'

She chose the brandy, unscrewed the cap and started to pour. But her hands shook and the liquid sloshed out too fast, hit the rim of the glass and splashed onto the sideboard. She cursed, the mishap pushing her to the verge of ridiculous tears, and then Nico's hand was closing over hers. Without a word, he removed the bottle from her grip and poured a generous measure into each tumbler.

Feeling foolish, she took the glass he handed her and tried to ignore the lingering effect of his touch. It was the same hot, static-like sensation she'd experienced at the gallery, when he'd crouched in front of her and taken her hand in his. Except his touch then had lasted longer, she recalled, and his thumb had rubbed gentle, delicious circles on the back of her hand, setting off a chain reaction of tiny sparks under her skin.

She took a gulp of brandy and welcomed its distracting burn. 'I don't understand,' she blurted when the heat had abated. 'Why me?' It was a question with no logical answer, she knew. She threw up a hand in helpless frustration. 'Your company provides protection services to public figures,' she said. 'You must know something about this sort of thing. Why would he go to such lengths to get my attention and yet keep his identity a secret?'

Nico stood with one hand wrapped around his glass, the other shoved in his trouser pocket. He paused, as if carefully weighing his response. 'In his mind, he's courting you, and he wants total control over this stage of his fantasy,' he said finally. 'The longer he remains anonymous, the more time he has to build the perfect relationship with you in his head and avoid the risk of real-life rejection.'

Marietta grimaced. 'That is totally twisted.'

Nico knocked back his brandy in a single swallow that made the muscles in his strong throat visibly work. 'I agree,' he said, then put the glass down and pulled his mobile phone from his pocket.

'Who are you calling?'

'Bruno, the police—' he tapped the screen and pressed the phone to his ear '—and your brother.'

Marietta sighed. *Eccellente.* An army of men was about to invade her beloved home. She chafed at the intrusion—at the very knowledge that she could no longer handle this situation by herself—but, loath as she was to admit it, she had no choice. She'd have to accept help.

Her brother arrived first, and he must have driven like a madman to complete the journey from his office in less than twenty minutes. He looked like a madman, too, with his tie skewed, his hair on end, his handsome face creased with worry—an expression that grew considerably darker the moment he looked in her bedroom.

'I'm fine,' she told him as he tipped up her chin and searched her face with dark, probing eyes. His jaw clenched, as if he didn't trust himself to speak, then he simply dropped a kiss on her head and stalked across the room to Nico.

Shortly afterwards, Bruno turned up, with a thin middle-aged man he introduced as a private forensic specialist, and, surreal though it all seemed, her lovely peaceful home began to resemble an official crime scene.

Marietta reached again for the brandy bottle and refilled her glass. She'd suffered through countless indignities during the painstaking months of rehabilitation and therapy after her accident, but this was a violation beyond her experience—beyond anything she'd equipped herself to deal with.

And it was so unfair—even though she knew life *was* unfair. Life didn't owe her anything. Which was why she had worked so hard for everything she had: her job at the gallery, which provided a steady income, the loft she'd bought and turned into a nice little earner by converting it into an art studio and hiring out the space to working artists, and her own art career—which, with a few exhibitions of her paintings and some lucrative commissions under her belt, was finally taking off.

Admittedly she'd accepted some help from Leo in the early days, but she'd repaid him every euro she'd borrowed—despite his vociferous protests. While her dear brother had never understood his little sister's need to assert her independence, he had finally accepted it.

She looked around at her apartment, filled with strangers. For years she'd prided herself on her strength and resilience, but she didn't feel at all strong and resilient today. She felt helpless and afraid and she hated it. Her gaze travelled across the room to where her brother and Nico stood by the window, deep in conversation, their dark heads bowed. Leo had already swooped in like a man possessed, bent on taking control. How long before he tried to smother her in a suffocating blanket of protectiveness?

And then there was Nico. A man so commanding, so authoritative, she imagined the world would stop on its axis if he so ordered it.

As though sensing her scrutiny, the men stopped talking and looked up, two sets of eyes—one midnight-dark, the other a startling blue—settling on her. At once unease bubbled up inside her. She didn't like the looks on their faces. Didn't like the determined set of Nico's jaw or the hint of something too much like apology in Leo's eyes.

Marietta lifted the brandy she'd poured without spilling a drop this time and took a large, fortifying gulp.

Those expressions told her the men had decided something—and she wasn't going to like it.

* * *

Nico had lied. First to Marietta and then, by omission, to her brother. Her stalker *had* left a note, and it was now in the hands of the forensic technician who was under strict orders to keep it out of sight. Leo already looked white-lipped and murderous. If he saw the sexually explicit language in the card he would undoubtedly lose the tight rein he held on his temper.

And Marietta—well, she'd already seen more than Nico had intended her to, thanks to a stubborn streak as wide as the Atlantic. Why she couldn't have simply obeyed him and stayed put, he couldn't fathom. Most of the time women were eager to please him, not defy him, and yet Marietta seemed to have a unique talent for the latter.

He handed his friend a double shot of whisky and Leo tossed the liquid down his throat, then glared at the empty glass as if he'd like nothing more than to smash it against a wall.

'How the hell did he get in?'

Guilt sliced through Nico's gut like a jagged knife. He'd failed to anticipate this turn of events. Failed to predict accurately the threat to Marietta's safety. Not least of all, he'd failed his friend.

And Nico didn't *do* failure—not on any scale. He had tasted that bitter elixir ten years ago and his failure then had cost him his wife's life.

He jammed his fists in his pockets. Focused his

thoughts with the same ruthless discipline that had seen him survive that brutal plunge into darkness and come out the other side—eventually.

'The windows don't appear to have been tampered with.' He gestured with his chin to the secured latch on the window by which they stood. 'My guess is he took an old-fashioned approach and picked the lock on the front door.'

'And the building?' Leo's scowl darkened. 'It should be secure twenty-four-seven.'

'He could have talked his way in.' Tension bit deep into Nico's shoulders. *He* had gained access the same way; it had been appallingly easy. 'Or waited and slipped in behind someone.'

'Dio.' Anger billowed from Leo in palpable waves. 'This is insane. What did the *polizia* say?'

Nico balled his hands more tightly in his pockets. The attitude of the two plain-clothes officers who had turned up at the apartment had reeked of apathy. 'They'll file a report, but don't expect too much action from that quarter,' he warned. 'They're viewing it as a romantic prank, at worst.'

Nico hadn't missed their exchange of lascivious grins over the lingerie and he'd wanted to knock the officers' heads together, plant his boot firmly in the seats of their pants. Just as he'd wanted to kick *himself* earlier, when he and Marietta had been in her bedroom and his thoughts had gone to a dark, carnal place they'd had no right to go. Not with Marietta. She was a victim, he'd had to remind himself, a woman who needed his help—and wondering how her ample breasts would look encased in that barely there bra had been wrong on too many levels to count.

Leo swore now—a vicious expletive that drew not so much as a blink from Nico. Five years in the French Foreign Legion as a young man, followed by several stints as a private military contractor, working alongside war-hardened ex-soldiers, had broadened his vocabulary to include every filthy word and crude expression known to man in half a dozen languages.

'Find him, Nico,' Leo grated, his expression fierce. 'Do whatever you have to to keep her safe.'

Do whatever you have to.

Those five words seemed to strike Nico in the gut one by one, like the consecutive blows of a steel mallet, and they left him savagely winded. He'd heard those same words before, ten years ago, from his former father-in-law's mouth.

Do whatever you have to.

And Nico had.

He'd utilised every resource within his power. Called in every favour owed him. Employed every conceivable tactic within the law—and beyond—to get Senator Jack Lewisham's daughter back.

But it wasn't enough. It all went belly up. And

Nico committed one critical, unforgivable sin: he underestimated the men who had taken her.

He failed. Failed to bring the senator's daughter home. Failed to save his wife's life.

Her father, who'd only grudgingly accepted Nico as a son-in-law in the first place, was inconsolable— a man irreparably broken by the loss of his only daughter.

He had not spoken to Nico since.

Do whatever you have to.

He glanced over at Marictta, nursing her brandy in her hand, quietly studying them. She was pale, but beautiful, those dark, intelligent eyes sizing him up. No doubt she was a little annoyed that she was not privy to his and Leo's conversation. She was a woman of undeniable strength, yet the pallor of her skin, the obvious tension around her eyes and mouth, belied her show of composure. He could see it in the rigid set of her shoulders, her too-tight grip on the glass, the unblinking wideness of her eyes.

Marietta wasn't afraid.

She was petrified.

Nico turned back to Leo, an idea seeding, taking shape in his mind. An extreme idea, perhaps, for it would mean sacrificing the sanctity of his personal space for a time, but extreme circumstances called for extreme measures. He clamped a hand over his friend's shoulder. 'Do you trust me, *mon ami*?'

Leo looked him in the eye. 'Of course,' he said

at once, his voice gruff. 'You do not need to ask me that, Nicolas.'

Nico nodded. It was the answer he'd hoped for. *'Très bien,'* he said. 'I have a suggestion.'

CHAPTER THREE

'ABSOLUTELY NOT!'

Marietta looked from her brother to Nico and back to Leo. *They had to be joking.* Yet neither man wore an expression she could describe as anything other than deadly serious. They both looked stern, formidable, standing side by side with their feet planted apart, their arms folded over their broad chests. Looking at them was akin to seeing double, and she wanted to slap them both.

'Pazzo!' she cried, gesturing with one hand in the air to emphasise just how crazy she found their proposal.

They had the gall to stare at her then, as if *she* were crazy. As if the idea of disappearing to some island off the coast of France until her stalker had been caught was the perfect solution and they couldn't understand why she didn't agree.

And not just *any* island.

Oh, no.

Nico's island.

Nico's *home.*

With Nico.

Heat that had nothing to do with anger and everything to do with the idea of being holed up on a remote island with Nicolas César scalded her insides.

Torture. That was what it would be. Exquisite torture of a kind she didn't dare contemplate.

She swigged down her brandy, set the glass on the sideboard and wheeled towards her kitchen. Enough alcohol. *Coffee.* That was what she needed. An injection of caffeine to hone her senses—and her tongue—for the showdown she was about to have with her brother.

He followed, his dark mood like a gathering thundercloud at her back.

'Marietta, just stop for a minute and think about this.'

'I don't need to stop in order to think.' She yanked the lid off a tin of coffee beans, unleashing a rich, nutty aroma that failed to please her the way it normally did. 'I'm a woman, so I can multitask, and I *am* thinking about it. I'm thinking what a stupid, *stupid* idea it is.'

She ignored his heavy sigh.

'You can't do this,' she ploughed on, pouring a handful of dark beans into her cherished *caffè* machine—her first port of call in the mornings, when strong coffee was a prerequisite for coherent speech.

'You can't just sweep in here and go all Big Brother on me. I'm not a rebellious, out-of-control teenager any more. I'm thirty years old. You're not responsible for me.'

An abrupt silence fell.

Marietta spun her chair around, regret, hot and instant, welling in her throat. 'Leo, I... I'm sorry.'

His jaw tightened. 'I will always feel responsible for you.'

'I know.'

Instantly she hated herself for hitting that sensitive nerve—the one that had been flayed raw by her accident thirteen years ago and had never completely healed. Leo blamed himself. Believed he should have tried harder to keep her at home that night.

The truth was no one could have saved Marietta except herself. *She* was the one who had sneaked out of the tiny flat she and Leo had shared. *She* was the one who'd gone to the party he'd expressly forbidden her to attend. *She* was the one who'd climbed into the back seat of a car with an inebriated driver.

Her decisions that night had borne consequences she had no choice but to live with, but the hell she had put her brother through was a heavy cross she would always bear.

The last of her temper dissolved. Leo loved her... wanted to keep her safe. How could she stay angry with him over that?

'I can't just drop everything and disappear.' She

tried for a softer, more reasonable tone. 'I have a job. Responsibilities. And Ricci's party is a week from tomorrow. Helena's had it planned for months. What if this guy hasn't been caught by then?' She shook her head. 'I can't stay away indefinitely—and I won't miss my nephew's first birthday.'

Leo crossed his arms, perched his lean frame on the edge of her low granite bench. 'Your life could be in danger, Marietta. Have you considered that?'

Now she wanted to roll her eyes, accuse him of being melodramatic—but *was* he? What had happened today felt serious, even if the *polizia* were inclined to view it as a prank. And after today's performance who could predict what kind of sick encore her stalker had planned?

A dull throb started up behind her eyes and she pressed her thumb and forefinger against her lids.

'When you cannot eliminate the source of danger your best defence is to remove yourself from its path.'

Nico's deep voice rumbled into the room and she jerked her hand down from her face. He loomed in her kitchen doorway, his sheer presence so commanding, his physique so powerful, that for a moment she couldn't help but feel a sense of reassurance—of safety—steal over her.

Still. That didn't change anything.

She couldn't put her life on hold indefinitely.

'A week, Marietta,' Leo urged. 'Give Nico a week.'

She looked at Nico. 'And how exactly are you going to catch my stalker if you're on an island with me?'

'I have faith in my people. He's upped the ante and so will we.'

'And if I insist on staying in Rome?'

'Then I'll appoint a bodyguard who'll shadow you day and night, wherever you go.'

'And I will stay,' Leo said. 'For as long as necessary.'

No. She gave an adamant shake of her head. 'You can't, Leo. It wouldn't be fair to Helena—or Ricci. You should be in Tuscany with them this weekend, not babysitting me.'

He shrugged. 'They'll come to Rome.'

Marietta pressed her fingertips to her temples. She knew her sister-in-law well. Helena was a kind, capable woman who wouldn't hesitate to uproot her domestic idyll for Marietta's sake. But Marietta's conscience wouldn't allow it. This was *her* problem to handle. How could she justify disrupting their lives when she had an alternative?

A week. Could she forego her independence, abandon her life, for a week? She looked at her brother and saw the deep lines of worry etched into his face. Her safety would give him peace of mind and didn't she owe him that much? He'd made so many sacrifices when they were younger, worked himself ragged to give them both a chance at a better life.

Doing what he asked of her now seemed a small thing in return.

She pushed her hands through her hair. Released her breath on a long sigh. '*Si*. Okay,' she said. 'One week.'

Marietta sat in the front passenger seat of her brother's car the next morning and chewed the inside of her cheek, fighting the powerful urge to blurt out that she'd changed her mind and all this was too sudden, too unexpected, and she couldn't possibly travel at short notice like this. Travel—for her—required careful planning, special considerations, and they hadn't given her a chance to plan a damned thing.

'Quit fretting, *carina*.' Leo glanced over, then returned his attention to negotiating the chaotic morning traffic. Even on a Saturday Rome's roads were flat-out crazy. 'Nico has everything under control.'

She cast him a sideways look. 'Will you stop doing that?'

'What?'

'Reading my mind.'

He grinned. 'If I knew the secret to reading women's minds, I would be a very rich man indeed.'

Had Marietta been in the mood for banter she would have reminded her brother that he *was* a rich man. Instead she turned her gaze out through the side window and watched the blur of busy streets and *piazze* and sidewalk cafés go by. She believed

Leo when he said his friend had everything under control—and that was the problem. Nico had all the control and she had none. It made her feel adrift, somehow. Alienated from her life. She didn't even know where exactly in the Mediterranean they were going. Until yesterday she'd never heard of Île de Lavande.

She rested her head against the soft leather seat.

Island of Lavender.

At least the name was pretty.

Perhaps she'd find some inspiration there for her next series of paintings? The European summer was in its twilight, but Nico had said the island was still warm, so she'd gone light on clothes and made room for packing her brushes and a set of fast-drying acrylic paints, a sketchpad and a small canvas. She'd even squeezed in a collapsible easel.

She supposed a few quiet, uninterrupted days of sketching and painting wouldn't be so bad—but only a few. She'd agreed to a week, no longer, and she still planned to be back in time for little Ricci's party. Nico's men would just have to pull out all the stops to find her stalker, because she wasn't compromising on that.

As for the gallery—she'd made two phone calls from Leo's apartment last night: one to her boss, the owner of the gallery, who'd expressed her support and understanding once apprised of the circumstances, and the other to Lina, who'd assured

Marietta that everything would run smoothly in her absence.

Too soon, the powerful car decelerated and the runway of the Aeroporto dell'Urbe came into sight. They drove through a security checkpoint and then they were on the Tarmac, headed for a sleek silver and black jet with the circular logo of César Security emblazoned on its tail.

Nico appeared in the open hatchway and Marietta leaned forward in her seat for a better view of the aircraft—and him.

And, *mamma mia*, he looked good. Faded jeans clung to long, muscular legs, he wore an untucked, open-necked white shirt, and a pair of dark shades obscured those deep blue eyes. His dark brown hair was stylishly mussed and his angular jaw sported a layer of stubble that only exaggerated his masculine appeal. He looked less formidable than yesterday. More relaxed, despite the ever-serious expression he wore.

Edible, an inner voice whispered, and she felt her face flame. *Santo cielo!* Her mind was *not* going there.

He jogged down the steps with an easy masculine grace, and he was pulling open the car door before her cheeks had even had time to cool. He hunkered down beside her.

'*Bonjour*, Marietta.' He removed his sunglasses

and the impact of that blue gaze arrowed all the way to her stomach. 'Are you ready for our journey?'

The morning breeze ruffled his hair and carried into the car the scent of soap and lemons, along with something more earthy and rich. Marietta tried not to breathe in, but the need for air prevailed. She frowned, growing more irritable by the second. No man should smell that enticing. That delectable.

'Do you have half-decent coffee on board?'

A muscle quirked at the side of his mouth—a mere flicker of movement that might have turned into a smile if he'd allowed it.

Had she ever seen Nico smile? It occurred to her that she hadn't—not properly.

'The coffee is *exceptionnel*,' he said, and she wished he wouldn't speak French.

It did squishy things to her insides and there was nothing good about squishy. *Nothing*.

He slid his shades back on. 'There's a lift on standby if you want it.'

She shook her head. '*Grazie*, but Leo will carry me on,' she said, preferring that simple, no-fuss solution over the mechanical platform that could raise her, wheelchair and all, to the door of the plane. Besides the ground crew there were few people around, but all the same she hated anything that created a spectacle or shone a spotlight on her disability. People often stared without meaning to, and though she'd grown inured to the curiosity of others, occasionally the attention still bothered her.

Minutes later her luggage was stowed and she was settled in a large, soft leather seat, her wheelchair reassembled and within reach should she wish to move about the plane's roomy interior once they were airborne. Out on the Tarmac, Nico and Leo exchanged final words. A moment before, when Leo had kissed her goodbye, silly tears had pricked the backs of her eyes, and she blinked now to clear her vision, annoyed because she rarely allowed herself to cry. She'd taught herself to be strong, to handle whatever challenges life threw at her, and all *this*— this was just another obstacle to overcome.

'I hear you're after some good, strong coffee, honey.'

Evelyn, the flight attendant who'd earlier introduced herself and then disappeared to give Marietta and Leo privacy, stood now by Marietta's seat, her cherry-red lips stretched into a friendly smile.

Marietta pulled herself together and looked up at the slender uniformed blonde. '*Si. Grazie.* Black and very strong, please.'

Not how she'd have ordered coffee in a bar in Rome—requesting a *caffè* in Italy automatically got you what the rest of the world labelled espresso— but Evelyn wasn't Italian, and Marietta wasn't in the mood for weak, watery coffee.

Evelyn tilted her head. '*Un caffè ristretto?*'

Marietta felt her brows climb and the other woman laughed. It was a pleasant laugh. Bubbly and bright.

'I know.' Evelyn winked. 'Who'd have thought a gal from Mississippi would know how to make proper Italian coffee.'

Marietta couldn't hold back a smile. 'You just improved my morning.'

Another long-lashed wink. 'My pleasure, honey. One coffee coming up,' she said, and Marietta decided right then that she liked Evelyn. Very, very much.

A short while later they were airborne. An hour after that they were cruising at forty-one thousand feet above sea level, halfway between Rome and their destination of Toulon, on the southern coast of France. Marietta knew this because Evelyn was a veritable fount of information. Unlike Nico who, aside from enquiring about her comfort prior to take-off, had uttered scarcely a word in the time since.

He sat in one of the cushioned club-style seats on the other side of the cabin, facing in her direction, so that if he looked up from his laptop they could easily converse. He hadn't. Not once in the last sixty minutes. Which made the challenge of snagging his attention almost impossible to resist.

'Here you go, honey.'

Evelyn placed a glass and the bottle of mineral water Marietta had asked for on the shiny walnut table in front of her. Marietta smiled her thanks. The *honey* might have sounded patronising from anyone else. From the tall, statuesque American it was just part of her charm.

Marietta watched her return to the other end of the cabin. It had to be an exciting life, jetting around the globe. Evelyn wore no rings, so presumably she was single, free of ties. Marietta didn't doubt she worked hard, but the perks had to be rewarding.

She waited until Evelyn was out of earshot before speaking. 'I like her.'

Nico's head came up and in her mind Marietta did a little self-congratulatory air-punch. Finally she had his attention.

'Pardon?'

'Evelyn,' she said, and watched to see his reaction. Because he had to know how beautiful his flight attendant was. No man could fail to notice a pair of legs as long and toned as Evelyn's, never mind that everything else about her was flawless and elegant.

Though Marietta felt sordid even thinking it, she couldn't help but wonder what level of 'personal service' Evelyn gave her boss. They were two beautiful people in the prime of their lives; they *had* to be aware of each other. Evelyn embodied the kind of physical perfection a man like Nico would no doubt look for in a sexual partner.

And yet he was frowning at her as if he hadn't a clue what—or whom—she was talking about.

'Your flight attendant,' she said, and stared at

him, astonished. 'You don't *know* the names of your flight crew?'

He shrugged. 'I have many hundreds of employees,' he said, his tone implying that he considered that a perfectly adequate excuse—and then he returned his attention to his computer.

End of conversation.

Marietta sniffed. 'Well, I like her,' she said to the top of his head. 'She's very good at her job. And she has spectacular legs.'

That got his attention back.

He looked at her and she shrugged. 'I'm an artist,' she said. 'I appreciate beauty in all its forms. And you have to admit Evelyn has great legs.'

'I hadn't noticed.'

'Really?' Her voice rang with disbelief.

'Oui,' he said, holding her gaze for a drawn-out beat. 'Really.'

And then something happened that she wasn't prepared for. His gaze dropped. First to her mouth, where it lingered for several seconds—long enough to make her self-consciously moisten her lips—and then down to her chest, where it rested only briefly. And yet the effect of that very deliberate scrutiny was so shocking, so profound, he might as well have touched her.

Heat prickled over her skin, from her neck to her breasts, and her heart pounded so hard, her pulse beat like the wings of a moth trapped in her throat.

Then his gaze came back to her face and she knew he must see the heightened colour there. One side of his mouth did that flickering thing again. That quirk that wasn't quite a smile.

'I'm a breast man myself,' he said, as casually as if he'd said he preferred beans over peas, or his steak medium rare, and then he went back to his work as if the air all around them *wasn't* sizzling and popping in the wake of that brief, electrifying exchange.

Marietta pressed her lips together. *Touché*, she conceded silently. Because shocking her into silence had no doubt been his intent. She uncapped her mineral water, filled her glass and took a long swig. But the cool liquid didn't douse the heat in her cheeks. Or the embarrassment washing through her. She had pushed him—deliberately provoked a reaction. Because... *Why?* Because she was bored? Because she felt ignored? Because Nico was the most beautiful, aloof man she'd ever met and some needy, feminine part of her craved his attention?

Oh, now, *that* did not sit well.

Marietta did not need a man's attention. She did not need a man, full stop. Her body might be broken beyond repair, but she had rebuilt her life regardless and it was everything she wanted. Everything she needed. Her job, her success as an artist...it was enough. It had to be enough.

Because she was done with wanting things she

would never have. Things that couldn't be. Things that were simply not written in her destiny.

You are a realist.

And Nico... Nico was just a fantasy.

CHAPTER FOUR

THE WEATHER IN Toulon was clear when they circled in for landing, the bright blue of the sky stretching as far as the eye could see along the Côte d'Azur, enhancing the beauty of a coastline that was coveted by holidaymakers and frequented year-round by the world's famous and rich.

Nico had no interest in the glamorous beaches and glittering nightlife that gave the French Riviera its reputation as a decadent playground. Toulon featured on his itinerary several times a year only because it was the nearest mainland airport to Île de Lavande, the quiet, secluded home he retreated to when he wasn't residing in Paris or New York or travelling across continents for business.

On occasion, however, when his mind grew restless and his body demanded a certain kind of release, he'd linger on the mainland for a night and venture into a glitzy casino or high-end bar. He'd order a shot or two of something—whatever he fancied on the night—and wait for them to come. And they always did. Those women with no hidden agendas who, like him, were simply looking for a good time. He would choose one—only ever one…gluttony wasn't his thing—and take her to a luxury hotel suite, order champagne and anything else she desired from the menu and let her flirt and tease for a while if that was her wont.

But not for too long.

He could be a gentleman when he chose, but he was no saint. Not when his thoughts were dark and his body primed and the only way to obliterate his memories was by losing himself in the pleasure of soft flesh and tight, wet heat.

Sometimes, if the sex was outstanding, he'd take a number, hook up with the same woman again, even indulge in the occasional dinner or outing. But only if she understood that pleasure was the only offer on the table. He had nothing more to give. Nothing beyond the physical certainly.

Julia had been his one love.

His one chance at a normal, happy life.

He didn't deserve another. Didn't want another only to have it brutally torn from him.

The jet touched down and he channelled his thoughts back to the present as they taxied to a stop on a private strip of Tarmac, close to where his helicopter awaited. He released his seat belt and stood, glancing over to where Marietta sat, as silent now as she'd been for the last hour of the flight.

He still didn't really know what their conversation in the air had been about. He'd wasted no time shutting it down, sensing it was going nowhere good, nowhere *safe*, but in so doing he'd spiked his awareness of her, and that awareness was still humming in his body like an electric current he couldn't switch off.

Was she upset with him? Hard to tell. Her gaze was focused out of the large oval window so that all he could see was her proud, elegant profile. *Dieu*, but she was lovely. High cheekbones. Straight nose. Flawless skin. Hair like burnished mahogany. And her lips were soft and full—ripe for tasting.

He clenched his jaw. *Not helpful.*

'Marietta?'

He half hoped she *was* annoyed. A little reserve, a touch of coolness between them, might be a good thing. He had one objective and that was to keep her safe. This spark of attraction he felt—there was no room for it.

She turned her head then and his hopes met a swift end. She didn't look angry. Didn't even look mildly irritated. Hell, she was *smiling* at him.

'Are we flying to the island in that?'

For a moment he didn't register the question, blindsided as he was by that smile. The pretty flush on her cheekbones. The breathless quality to her voice that seemed to stroke right into him.

She looked out through the window again and he leaned down, followed the line of her gaze to where his chopper sat on the Tarmac, its long rotor blades and black paintwork gleaming in the sunshine. A man in blue overalls and a fluorescent orange vest moved around the craft, completing a thorough safety check that Nico himself would repeat prior to take-off.

'*Oui,*' he said. 'The island is accessible by boat, but the chopper is faster.'

'I've never been in a helicopter.' Her gaze swung to his. 'Will you pilot it?'

'Of course.'

She fired another look out of the window and then undid her seatbelt and smoothed the creases from her grey linen pants. 'Okay. I'll wait here while the luggage and my wheelchair are transferred,' she said, her voice turning brisk. 'Take me last.'

'There's a lift—'

'No,' she cut across him. 'No fuss. Please.' Her gaze didn't quite meet his. 'It will be quicker and easier if you carry me.'

Easier, Nico reflected ten minutes later as he settled Marietta into the cockpit of the chopper, was a relative term. Because the effort of willing his groin not to harden in response to holding a soft, warm woman in his arms—a woman who smelled enticingly of strawberries and vanilla and something faintly exotic—had not come anywhere close to being easy.

He strapped her into the harness, made a couple of adjustments that brought his fingers dangerously, agonisingly close to her breasts, then hastily withdrew his hands.

'Comfortable?' She nodded and he handed her a black helmet. 'This has a built-in headset so we can communicate. I need to do a final weather check and then we're set.'

Her gaze turned skyward. 'The weather looks perfect.'

'*Oui*. But we're flying twenty miles south over open sea. The marine winds can be unpredictable.'

Rather like his body, he thought grimly.

Marietta's heart raced and she gripped the edges of her seat. She looked down at the deep, surging swells of the Mediterranean Sea, then up again to the lone mass of land looming in the distance. Silhouetted against a bright blue sky, the island's long, uneven shape teased her imagination and made her think of a great serpent slumbering on the horizon.

She'd always wanted to fly in a helicopter and now she was hurtling over the ocean in one and struggling to hold back a grin. Which was crazy. What reason did she have to smile or feel breathless and giddy?

Yesterday her life had been turned upside down, her home invaded by a man who at worst was a predator and at best was a disturbed individual in dire need of a shrink. Yet somehow, right at this moment, all of that seemed very distant and she really was fighting an insane urge to grin.

She let her gaze roam the cockpit's interior, fascinated by the dials and buttons and levers. Beside
her, Nico looked at home in the pilot's seat, his large
hands working the controls of the powerful machine
with dexterity and ease.

Strong hands, she thought, recalling how he'd
carried her from the jet to the helicopter as if she
weighed next to nothing. As if carrying a woman
was something he did every day and the experience
left him unaffected. While *she* had been hyper-aware
of *everything*. From the hardness of his body and the
citrusy scent of his cologne to the tanned triangle of
chest in the opening of his shirt and the glimpse of
dark hair at the base of that V.

She'd wondered whether the texture of that hair
was soft or coarse. If it thickened and spread across
his chest or was merely a dusting. If it arrowed into
a fine line that bisected his stomach and travelled
into the waistband of his pants and lower.

Inappropriate thoughts she should not have had
then and should not be having now. Not about the
man she was going to spend the next few days
cooped up with on an island.

She dragged her attention off his hands and back
to the mass of land ahead of them that was appearing
more substantial by the second. Running her gaze
along the nearest stretch of coastline, she made out
three separate white sand beaches and, nestled into
the lee of a lush hill range, a large village and a port,

where rows of colourful boats were moored to long wooden wharves jutting into clear turquoise waters.

'You own a whole *village*?'

A short burst of static came over the headset before the rich timbre of Nico's voice filled her helmet. It was an odd sensation—as if he was inside her head and all around her at the same time.

'No. I own sixty percent of the island, including the southern and western coasts. The rest—including the northern beaches, the olive groves to the east and a small commercial vineyard—is now owned by various locals whose families have lived on Île de Lavande for hundreds of years.'

'*Now* owned?' she said. 'Did they not always own it?'

'*Non.* For several centuries the island was owned by a single aristocratic French family. They employed caretakers and servants who settled on the land with their families. It wasn't until a wealthy American industrialist bought the island in the early nineteen-hundreds and decided to sell off some parcels of land that the locals finally had the opportunity to become landowners instead of leaseholders.'

Fascinated, she took a moment to absorb it all. 'How do the islanders make their living? Fishing?'

'*Oui.* And from olives and wine. Most of which they sell to the mainland. Plus a controlled level of tourism.'

'Controlled?'

'Limited numbers of tourists, and only at certain times of the year. During those months a passenger and car ferry visits twice a week—no more. The villagers rely on the revenue, but they also want to protect the environment—and their privacy.'

'Are most of them descended from the original settlers?'

'Many of them, *oui*.'

'That must be amazing—to know the history of generations of your family.' Silence crackled in her headset. 'Do you have any familial links to the island?' she asked.

'*Non,*' he said.

'So…you have family living in France?'

'*Non.*'

The message in that second abrupt no was clear. *Subject off-limits*. Marietta bit down on her tongue— and her curiosity—and focused on the scenery.

Ahead, an old sturdy fishing vessel rode the ocean swells as it chugged slowly into the calmer waters of the harbour. Nico flew the chopper directly over the boat, low enough to see the broad smiles on the fishermen's upturned faces. They raised their arms and waved and Nico waved back—and Marietta's surprise lasted only a second. Mr Security Conscious *would* know his neighbours, she realised. Even a whole village of them.

They neared land and he banked the helicopter to the right, angling them over the port and the outskirts of the village. She glimpsed red-tiled roofs and open shutters on whitewashed houses, an old stone church and the crumbling remains of a sprawling derelict structure on the crest of a hill.

'Where's your home?'

'Further around the coast,' he said. 'Twenty-five minutes by road from the port.'

The village fell behind them and she looked down, saw rows upon rows of pine trees extending into the island's interior. It was lush and dense—much more fertile and beautiful than she'd expected.

'Will you show me some of the island while we're here?'

'Perhaps. If time allows. We have work to do first.'

She turned her head to look at him. 'What kind of work?'

'Questions and answers.'

Her brows knitted. 'I don't understand...'

'We are going to dissect your life, Marietta. Day by day. Hour by hour. Minute by minute. You are going to break down every routine for me—everything you do, everywhere you go, everyone you meet—until we have ruled out the possibility that your stalker is someone you know or have met.'

A groan rose in her throat. 'But I've answered all of Bruno's questions. *And* yours.'

'And you will answer them again,' he said. 'As many times as I need you to. Until I am satisfied.'

His tone was uncompromising and a shiver rippled through her. *How ironic*. Yesterday she'd spared a thought for anyone unfortunate enough to find themselves interrogated by Nicolas César—soon she would experience for herself that very ordeal.

Her mood well and truly dampened, she stayed silent for the rest of the flight, even stifling her exclamation of *wow* when she spotted the house perched on a high plateau above a steep limestone cliff.

Sleek, white, and über-modern, the expansive single-level dwelling might have dominated its surroundings. Instead, its simple understated design complemented the landscape, with acres of glass reflecting the sky and the rich, fertile land all around it. On the ocean side a flat terrace featured a large swimming pool, which sparkled like a sheet of cobalt glass in the sunshine. On the inland flank, a circular courtyard sat at the head of a long winding driveway which descended into a thick forest of towering pines.

Marietta surveyed the property as Nico set them down on a dedicated helipad a short distance from the courtyard.

It was, she decided after a moment, just like its owner.

Stark. Remote. And beautiful.

CHAPTER FIVE

'ENOUGH!'

The shrill note in Marietta's voice brought Nico's head up. He laid his pen on the legal pad he used for old-fashioned note-taking and leaned back in his chair. 'Take a breath, Marietta.'

'Don't patronise me,' she snapped, a flash of Italian temper darkening her eyes to the colour of hot, bitter espresso. She squeezed them shut and pinched the delicate bridge of her nose.

Nico stretched out his denim-clad legs, crossed his bare feet at the ankles and waited for her to calm down.

'I'm sorry.' She dropped her hand, opened her eyes. 'I didn't mean to snap. I just don't see how where I choose to buy my fruit and vegetables on a Saturday morning can possibly be relevant.'

A warm, gentle Mediterranean breeze rippled the surface of the pool and swayed the enormous umbrella which shaded the outdoor table where they sat. Sighing, Marietta scraped her long hair back from her face and secured the lustrous swathe into a high ponytail which she fastened with an elastic band from her wrist.

Toying with his pen, Nico studied her. He couldn't detect a scrap of make-up on her this morning and still she was beautiful. 'More coffee?'

She nodded. 'Please.'

He refilled her cup from the heavy silver coffee pot his part-time housekeeper Josephine had set out for them, along with a selection of fruits, thick yoghurt, freshly baked croissants and homemade jams.

It had been good of Josephine to drive up from the village on a Sunday morning. She and her son Luc had already been at the house in the hours prior to Nico and Marietta's arrival, cleaning, stocking the kitchen and installing special handrails in the guest en-suite bathroom at Nico's request. He appreciated their commitment; he'd given them only a day's notice and yet they hadn't complained at a time when their family-run bistro had to be busy with the final late-summer run of tourists.

Josephine had said she'd returned this morning to check that everything was satisfactory, but Nico figured it was curiosity as much as solicitude that had brought her back. In the four years since he'd built his home on Île de Lavande, he'd never invited a guest there—had never allowed anyone inside his sanctuary aside from the select few he employed for its upkeep. In that respect Marietta was something of a novelty, and she had—not surprisingly—charmed his housekeeper.

It was a charm she had not extended to *him* for the last hour and a half, he noted dryly. He sat forward, picked up his pen. 'Tell me more about Davide,' he said, and watched her expression instantly shutter.

'There isn't much to tell. We had a relationship and then we broke up. End of story.'

'You were together for two years.' The same length of time he and Julia had been married. 'It must have been serious,' he said, ignoring the sudden sharp clench in his chest.

Her shoulders, bare aside from the straps of her pale blue tank top, hitched up. 'For a while, *si*.'

'Who broke it off?'

'I did.'

'Why?'

'That's personal.' She picked up her sunglasses from the table and pushed them onto her face. 'And if you think Davide could be my stalker, you're wrong. He's moved on. Married. Started a family. What is it the English say? You are barking into the wrong bush.'

His mouth twitched despite himself. 'Up the wrong tree.'

She flicked a hand in the air. 'Whatever. Anyway, it can't be Davide. The cards are always signed off with an *S*.'

He put down his pen again. Worked to keep the

impatience out of his voice. 'First, the *S* could stand for anything,' he said. 'Second, I know this is difficult, but any previous romantic partners must be considered as potential suspects until they've been definitively ruled out.'

Her graceful chin took on that stubborn tilt he was learning to recognise. 'How do you know my stalker isn't a complete stranger?'

'I don't. And I haven't discounted the possibility. But the majority of stalking victims are stalked by someone they know—two-thirds of female victims by a former or current partner.' He paused before driving home his point. 'It is extremely likely that you have met or know your stalker in some capacity. He could be your neighbour. Someone you've met through work. Maybe the guy who sells you fruit at the market on a Saturday morning.'

She shuddered visibly. '*Santo cielo.* It could be anyone.'

'*Exactement.* And the sooner we narrow the field of potential suspects, the closer we get to identifying the real perpetrator.'

She sat a little straighter in her wheelchair, pulled in a deep breath and slowly expelled it. 'Okay.' She folded her hands in her lap. 'What do you want to know about Davide?'

'How did he react when you ended the relationship?'

She hesitated. 'He was upset.'

'Angry?'

'A little,' she said, quietly. 'Mostly hurt, I think.'

'He didn't want it to end?'

She reached for her coffee, took a careful sip, then replaced the cup before answering. 'He'd asked me to marry him.'

Nico blinked.

'I know,' she said, before he'd fully processed that potentially critical piece of information. 'A perfectly normal, eligible, good-looking guy asks a crippled girl to marry him and she says no.' She laughed, but the sound wasn't at all pretty. 'You're thinking a girl like me can hardly afford to be choosy, right?'

A flash of anger—and perhaps indignation—snapped his brows down. 'That is not what I was thinking.'

'But you were thinking *something*,' she challenged.

He felt a pulse leap in his jaw. 'I was thinking you should have told me this sooner.'

'Is that all?'

'*Non,*' he said tersely. 'I was also thinking the poor bastard must have been crushed when you turned him down.'

Marietta's chin jerked back—with surprise or scepticism? He couldn't tell.

'Why did you reject his proposal?'

She picked up her coffee again, took another sip, as if buying time to compose herself. When she put the cup down her hand wasn't quite steady. 'Davide wanted to *fix* me.'

'What do you mean?'

'He was obsessed with the idea of curing me.'

'Your paralysis?'

'*Si.*'

He frowned. 'And that was a bad thing?'

'For me it was. It made our relationship untenable.'

'Why?'

Her slim shoulders lifted, dropped. 'Because I didn't share his obsession.'

Nico rubbed his jaw, assimilating that. 'So you don't believe in the possibility of a cure?'

A small groove appeared on her forehead. 'I believe there's hope for a cure. Technology and medicine will always advance, and people who are passionate about finding a way to reverse spinal cord damage will always be looking for the next major breakthrough. But at some point you have to stop chasing the miracle and get on with the business of living. And that means learning to accept the hand you've been dealt. Davide couldn't do that. He couldn't accept that I wouldn't one day get out of this chair and walk. Instead he spent every spare minute researching medical journals and the latest treatments he thought I should try.'

Marietta paused. She was glad suddenly that she'd put her sunglasses on, because if eyes truly were the windows to the soul she didn't want Nico seeing into hers. Didn't want him seeing the hidden part of her that still hurt whenever she thought about Davide and his obsession with 'fixing' her.

She might have shared his enthusiasm if she hadn't already travelled that same road with her brother in the early years after the accident, when Leo convinced himself—and her—that there was a real chance she would walk again. His tenacity and determination were contagious and she let herself get swept up in the possibilities—agreed, once Leo convinced her he could afford it, to travel to Germany and undergo the experimental treatments he'd researched.

But in the end it all turned into nothing more than a wild rollercoaster of shattered hopes and dreams. An enormous, heartbreaking reality check that devastated her for a time—until she picked herself up and fiercely told herself that from then on she was going to be a *realist*, not a dreamer.

And then, scarcely a year later, she met Davide and became that naive, hopeful fool all over again. The one who was stupid enough to think she could have something as ordinary as a husband and a family. The doctors had told her years before that she was physically capable of bearing children but she'd firmly quashed that dream—because what man would want to have a family with *her*?

But then Davide had come along, and at some point during their relationship she'd forgotten that *ordinary* didn't exist for her. That *ordinary* was a fantasy. That *ordinary* was something she had forfeited the night she'd climbed into the back seat of that car with her young, ill-fated friends.

'He said he loved me, but the woman he loved was the version of me in his head,' she said now, unable to stop a hint of bitterness creeping into her voice. 'The one he wanted to turn me into. The one who could walk.'

Nico shifted in his chair. 'Were you not tempted to consider any of the treatments?'

And now he was delving deeper than he needed to go. Deeper than he knew he should go. Finding Marietta's stalker and keeping her safe until then were his only concerns. He needn't care about anything else. Caring, he reminded himself, made people vulnerable, weak—and in his line of work, there was no room for weakness.

'I've been down that road,' she said. 'I had several surgeries and experimental stem cell procedures at a specialised clinic in Berlin. The results were negligible. A tiny bit of muscle movement, some increased sensation—that's all.'

'And Davide knew this?'

'*Si*. He said I gave up too easily.'

Nico's mouth settled into a grim line. She'd made the right decision to ditch the *imbécile*. Any man fool enough to label this woman a quitter didn't deserve her.

He closed the pad, pushed his chair back from the table. He would call Bruno, relay the information he deemed useful and tell him to take a closer look at the ex. Bruno had already compiled a superficial dossier on Davide, but now Nico would give the green light to dig deeper. Pay the guy a visit.

'We're done?' She sounded surprised. Or relieved. Maybe both.

He stood. 'For now,' he said, aware of something like relief coursing through his own veins.

These last two hours had been intense—for both of them—and he suddenly wanted some distance from this woman. Wanted her out of his sight so that he could concentrate on work and stop noticing things about her he had no legitimate need to notice.

Like the way those full lips of hers pursed when she was thinking and one cheek hollowed slightly, as if she were biting the inside of it. Or the way she sometimes used her hands to emphasise a point and at other times clasped them in her lap to give the impression of composure. Or the way she occasionally rubbed her shoulders or the back of her neck, as if the muscles there were cramped and needed loosening. Or—and this was by far the most disturbing of all his observations—how pink and delectable her tongue looked when it darted out to rescue a flake of croissant from her bottom lip.

Nico picked up the pen and pad and stepped back. *Oui*. Distance. A lot of it—and for the rest of the day, preferably. 'You did well, Marietta. Relax now. Enjoy the sunshine.'

She looked up and he saw his reflection in duplicate in her oversized sunglasses. 'What are you going to do?'

'Work.'

'All day?'

'Probably.' He turned towards the house. Pretended not to see the sudden slight pout on those voluptuous lips.

'What about sightseeing?'

He pulled up. 'Pardon?'

'Sightseeing,' she repeated. 'You said you would show me the island.'

He frowned. 'If time permitted.'

Her chin rose in that tenacious way of hers that stirred irritation and something much hotter, more dangerous, inside him.

'I've answered your questions,' she said.

He curled his fingers around the pen. 'My priority is to keep you safe until your stalker is caught, Marietta, not babysit you or play tour guide.' Her head drew back as if he'd spat in her face, but he ruthlessly fought the urge to soften his tone. 'Now, if you'll excuse me, I have work to do.'

He turned and strode into the house. Into his study. Where he tossed the pen and pad onto his desk with such force the pen pinwheeled across the glass surface and onto the floor.

Grunting, he leaned down to pick it up and told himself the burn he could feel deep in his gut was irritation.

Not an attack of conscience.

And *not* desire.

Marietta dropped her sketchpad and pencil onto the solid wooden table where she'd sat earlier with Nico and pulled out her earbuds, trading the orchestral tones of her classical playlist for the natural summer chorus of cicadas and the distant cries of gulls circling over the ocean.

She closed her eyes, breathed in the briny scent of the sea and the distinctive floral notes of the wild lavender that stained the island's clifftops a vibrant purple and gave Île de Lavande its name.

It was beautiful here, peaceful—a world away from the crazy pace and relentless noise of Rome—but the creative inspiration she'd hoped for had proved elusive and her efforts this afternoon had been disappointing, to say the least.

She was in the wrong headspace. Upset with Nico and more so with herself for letting him affect her like this. Allowing him to make her feel guilty and ungrateful simply because she wanted to see more of his beautiful island. She understood that he was busy. Understood that he must have had to rearrange his schedule to bring her here. But this outlandish idea had been *his*, not hers.

And she had tried to co-operate. Had tried to prevent her temper from flaring as she'd answered every personal, invasive question he'd fired at her.

He should not look so gorgeous. Should not have sat there in his worn jeans and his white T-shirt, with his feet bare and that film of dark stubble on his jaw that gave him a deliciously rough, disreputable edge. How could she concentrate with all that flagrant male energy swirling around her like a hot mist, drenching the very air she needed to breathe?

She opened her eyes and let her gaze drift beyond the terrace towards the clifftop and the blue expanse of sea that was so vast Marietta felt very insignificant all of a sudden, and for some reason very lonely.

Her brows tugged together.

Santo cielo.

What was wrong with her?

She didn't wallow like this.

She was strong—a battler like her *mamma* had been—not a dreamer given to fits of melancholy like her father, a man who had become so lost in his grief, so consumed by addiction, that he'd neglected his children and forced his son to assume the role of provider before he'd even reached his teens.

Looking back on those years always reminded her how lucky she had been to have Leo. She'd been only seven when their mother died, so Marietta's memories of her were limited, but she knew in her heart that Estelle Vincenti would have been proud of her son for stepping up.

And would she have been proud of you?

Marietta's frown sharpened as the question popped into her head. She liked to think her mother would have forgiven the fractious, rebellious teenager she'd been—the girl who'd acted out in the absence of a mother's love and influence—and regarded the woman she'd become with pride and affection.

Yet she would never know for certain the answer to that question, would she?

Her eyes prickled and she cursed.

Enough.

It was being stuck here on this remote estate with a man who clearly didn't wish to spend more time with her than was necessary that was plunging her into this funk. A friendly voice and distraction—that was what she needed. She turned her wheelchair and headed for the house. She'd call her sister-in-law, Helena, and see how the plans for Ricci's birthday party were coming along.

Except when Marietta reached the beautiful blue and white guest bedroom she'd been given and fished her mobile out of her bag, she discovered the phone was dead and realised she'd forgotten her charger.

She swore again, and wheeled out of the room. Had she seen a landline phone anywhere in this sprawling modern abode? She rolled along the wide hallway and paused outside the open door to the study where Nico had spent most of the afternoon. He'd emerged half an hour ago and declared that he was going for a short run. She'd pasted on a smile and waved him off as if she couldn't care less what he did.

She looked into the room. It was neat and masculine, with lots of sharp edges and straight lines, glass surfaces and sleek, pale wood. A textured black rug, a tan leather sofa and a matching desk chair were the only soft furnishings.

And on the glass-topped desk sat a phone.

More eager by the second to hear a familiar voice, she glided over to the desk and dialled her sister-in-law's mobile number.

'Helena,' she said a moment later. 'It's me.'

'Marietta!' Helena's posh English voice rushed down the line. 'I've been thinking about you all weekend. This whole business is just dreadful. Is everything all right over there? Is Nicolas treating you well?' A fleeting pause. 'He'd *better* be treating you well.'

Marietta smiled to herself. 'Everything's fine. A little quiet, that's all.'

She stared out of the large window which faced the terrace, her gaze trailing over the pool and the table where she'd sat drawing for much of the afternoon. Her brows pinched. Had Nico watched her from his desk while he'd worked?

'Tell me about Ricci's party,' she said, pushing aside that thought. 'How's the planning going?'

'Great. Except Leo is such a proud *papà* he's invited half of Tuscany—and Rome...'

Marietta was still smiling as she wound up the call, some ten minutes later. 'Give Ricci and Leo my love. I'll see you in six days.'

'Are you sure?'

'Of course. I'll be there,' she said firmly. 'I'm not missing Ricci's first birthday for anything.'

She hung up feeling lighter, less maudlin and more like herself. This ugly business of her stalker would be over soon and she'd have her life back. She reversed away from the desk, turned towards the door—and saw something against the wall on the far side of the doorway she hadn't noticed upon entering. It was a piece of antique furniture totally at odds with the rest of the decor and yet so lovely it commanded her attention for a long moment. She inched closer and recognised it was a vintage rolltop desk, crafted from a rich golden oak which gleamed as if someone had polished it only yesterday.

And, oh, it was *magnifico*. A stunning piece of craftsmanship her artist's eye couldn't fail to admire. Lured by its beauty, she brushed her hand over the intricate gold leaf designs on the drawer-fronts and fingered the little gold lock and key at the bottom of the tambour lid. She'd always adored the idea of these old-fashioned desks, with their hidden nooks and crannies, and before the left side of her brain could issue a caution she had turned the key and pushed up the slatted tambour to reveal the interior.

Immediately Marietta knew she had gone too far—gone somewhere she shouldn't have—because everything inside the desk…every item sitting in its neat, allotted space…was too pretty and feminine to belong to a man.

Unease flared, even as curiosity kept her gaze fixated. One of the central nooks accommodated a pretty peach-coloured writing compendium, with an elegant silver pen lying on top and a bright orange reading glasses case alongside it. In the next cubbyhole sat a large trinket box, fashioned from dark wood with mother-of-pearl inlay, and a smaller silver box with an ornamental lid. A neat stack of hardcover books filled another space, and below them a solid silver photo frame lay face-down on the desk's polished surface.

Don't look.

But the strident command in her head couldn't stay her hand. Her fingers stroked the velvet backing of the frame and then tilted it up. She stared at a photo of a much younger Nico, in profile, gazing adoringly at a striking golden-haired woman in a long white veil and wedding dress.

A door opening and closing, followed by the sound of footsteps and fast, rough breathing, catapulted Marietta's heart into her throat. The footsteps travelled down the hall, then retreated, and seconds later, through the window, she saw Nico emerge onto the terrace.

His back was to her but she could see he was breathing hard, his impressive shoulders lifting with each deep, controlled breath. His T-shirt stuck to his broad back and his running shorts emphasised narrow hips, a taut backside and long, muscular legs. He was hard and honed, every sweaty, musclebound inch of him, and for a few seconds Marietta lost all sense of her surroundings as some visceral response to all that hardcore virility short-circuited her brain and triggered a burst of heat in her belly and breasts.

He turned and strode into the house. 'Marietta?'

She jolted back to herself and looked at the photo, still in her hand. Gently, her fingers shaking a little, she replaced the frame. She'd wasted precious seconds and now it was too late to avoid discovery. She couldn't close up the desk with the necessary care—she'd never risk damaging this beautiful antique—and get out of the study undetected.

She clasped her hands in her lap and swallowed hard. She had trespassed, but not with any malicious intent. This was a minor transgression, she assured herself. She would own it.

'I'm in your office,' she called out.

He was there within seconds, and she saw on his face the exact moment he registered the raised lid of the desk. Saw his nostrils pinch and flare, his mouth flatten into a hard line, and knew with a sharp mix of certainty and regret that he wouldn't simply shrug off the intrusion.

His large body went still—so still it frightened her.

Her heart thundered in her ears. 'Nico, I'm sorry.' The apology spilled out in a breathless rush. 'I came in to use the phone and saw the desk and it was so beautiful... I... I didn't think.'

If possible his features grew tighter, his eyes harder. He said nothing, and the silence, broken only by his harsh breathing, was awful.

'I'm so sorry,' she said again, and her voice cracked. Because this time she wasn't only apologising for opening the desk. This time she was telling him she was sorry about his wife. She knew nothing about his marriage, of course, but the photograph, the desk so lovingly preserved—almost like a shrine—told her two things.

Nico had loved his wife.

And his wife was no longer alive.

Marietta's throat constricted. 'Please say something,' she whispered.

He moved to the desk, carefully lowered the lid and laid his palms on the tambour. He didn't look at her, and somehow that was ten times worse than his hard, silent stare.

'Go,' he said at last, and the command was all the more terrible for its quietness.

'Nico—'

'Get out, Marietta.'

Still he didn't look at her, and the rebuff needled deep, even though she knew she'd earned it. Smothering the impulse to apologise yet again, Marietta turned her chair and wheeled out of the room.

CHAPTER SIX

Nico walked out to the terrace with two crystal tumblers balanced in one hand and an unopened bottle of vintage cognac from the back of his liquor cabinet cradled in the other.

He paused. Marietta sat in her wheelchair at the table by the pool with her back to him, her slender form silhouetted by the dying light of the sun, which was now no more than a sliver of fiery orange on the horizon. Her long mahogany hair spilled in loose waves down her back, and before he could censor his thoughts he found himself wondering how it would feel to slide his fingers through those thick tresses, wind them around his hands...

He tightened his jaw. Shook off the thought as swiftly as it had surfaced. Marietta was his friend's sister and right now her safety was his responsibility. This incessant awareness of her was an unwelcome distraction and he needed to shut it down. At the very minimum he needed to control his thoughts and reactions around her—especially after today, when he had not reacted well to finding her at Julia's desk…had not known how to handle the unexpected gut-punch of emotion or the glitter of sympathy in Marietta's eyes.

Seeing the woman who'd lit a slow-burning fire in his blood these past forty-eight hours alongside the only mementoes he had of his dead wife had unbalanced him, had fired a shock wave through his brain that had stolen his ability to do more than clip out a few terse words.

And that look he'd seen on Marietta's face… Apology mixed with *pity*, of all things. His gut had hardened, everything within him rejecting that look. Rejecting the idea of Marietta feeling sorry for him. Of *anyone* feeling sorry for him. Nico elicited a range of reactions from people—respect, obedience, trust, fear—but rarely sympathy or pity. If ever. Witnessing both in Marietta's eyes had left him feeling sideswiped. Exposed. Something he had worked hard for the last decade *not* to feel. And yet even now, years later, he didn't always succeed in burying his feelings—did he? Occasionally the darkness would try to claim him. The guilt and the burning sense of failure that had dogged him ever since Julia's death would rise up and torment him.

He strode to the table and set down the bottle and glasses. He'd come out here to make peace, he reminded himself. Not to examine his inner workings.

Marietta looked up, her liquid dark eyes startled at first, then veiled and wary. One graceful eyebrow rose. 'Are we celebrating something?' She looked from the bottle to him. 'Perhaps you've caught my stalker and you're gracing me with your presence to tell me I can return to civilisation tomorrow?'

Nico let the sarcasm slide. He'd avoided her for much of the day and she was upset with him. Women didn't like to be ignored—he remembered that much from his too brief time as a married man. He took in her pale cotton pants, the soft green halterneck top which clung to her generous curves and left her golden shoulders exposed. Had she changed especially for dinner? A needle of guilt pricked him. She'd knocked on his study door an hour ago, offered to fix a meal for them, and he'd grunted a response through the closed door, telling her to eat without him.

He opened the bottle and poured a double shot of cognac into each tumbler, put one in front of Marietta and settled in a cushioned seat beside her. 'You do not consider Île de Lavande to be civilised?' He swirled the cognac in his glass. 'Or perhaps you are referring to the company?'

Colour crept into her cheeks but her chin stayed elevated. 'I'm sure parts of Île de Lavande are very civilised—I'm simply yet to see most of the island. As for the company—so far it's been…' She shrugged minutely. 'Satisfactory.'

Despite the tension in the air Nico felt his facial

muscles twitch, and then his lips were stretching into a rare smile. Had a woman ever described him as 'satisfactory' before? No. He didn't think so. On the infrequent occasions when he indulged in female company, he made damn sure the woman was a great deal more than *satisfied* when he was done with her.

He raised his glass. '*Touché*, Marietta.' He swallowed a mouthful of the expensive cognac and noted she hadn't touched hers. 'You are angry,' he observed.

'No...' she began, and then stopped, shook her head and puffed out a quiet sigh. '*Si*. A little,' she confessed. 'I made a mistake and you won't accept my apology. I'm angry with myself *and* with you.'

He lifted his eyebrows. 'That's a candid statement,' he said, which maybe shouldn't have surprised him. Marietta had never struck him as a smoke-and-mirrors kind of woman. She was headstrong and honest. Unafraid to speak her mind.

She reached out suddenly, and curled her hand around his wrist. 'I didn't mean to intrude, Nico,' she said softly. 'And I truly am sorry—about your wife.'

Heat radiated from her touch—a sharp, unsettling contrast to the inevitable icy chill that swept through him whenever he thought about his wife—and then she was sliding her hand away, sitting back.

'How long were you married?'

His chest grew uncomfortably tight. 'Two years.'

'She was very beautiful.'

So she *had* taken a good look at the photograph. He

didn't know how he felt about that. He took another generous sip of cognac, held the liquid in his mouth for a moment before letting it burn down his throat. He *did* know he wasn't going to have this conversation.

'Who did you call?' he asked, and the abrupt change of subject elicited an immediate frown.

'Scusi?'

'You said you went into my study to use the phone,' he reminded her. 'Who did you call?'

'My sister-in-law.'

'Because…?'

Her shoulders stiffened. 'Because I wanted to hear a friendly voice,' she said, her tone turning defensive, faintly accusing.

Nico cursed himself silently. He'd come out here to make peace, to defuse the tension between them before it sprouted claws—not to pick a fight. He had no wish to speak of his late wife, no desire to dredge up the darkness that lurked too close to the surface, but he could have deflected Marietta's curiosity in a less antagonistic manner.

'Forgive me,' he said, his voice gruff, the words alien on his tongue.

Rarely did he apologise or seek forgiveness. The last time had been ten years ago, the day of Julia's funeral, and on that day his father-in-law had been disinclined to forgive.

'You may call whomever you wish, whenever you wish,' he said. 'The house and its facilities are yours to use as you desire. However, I will ask one thing of you.' He held her gaze, kept his voice low. Measured. 'Please do not ever again speak of my wife.'

For a long moment Marietta's gaze didn't falter from his, then her lashes lowered, shielding her expressive eyes from him. She backed her chair away from the table.

'Understood,' she said, glancing up, her gaze reconnecting with his briefly. '*Buona notte*, Nico.'

And then she turned her chair around and wheeled into the house, leaving her drink sitting untouched on the table.

Nico watched her go and something pierced him. Something, he thought darkly, like regret. He reached for her glass, downed the double shot of cognac and scowled into the empty tumbler. That had *not* gone at all how he'd planned.

'It's not the ex-boyfriend, boss.'

Nico leaned back in his chair, his phone pressed to his ear. 'Are you positive?'

'Yes,' Bruno said. 'The guy was in Vienna on business all day Friday. And my gut says it's not him. He's settled, content. Devoted to his wife and kid. The wife's a looker, too.'

Nico ignored that last comment. He ran his hand through his hair, across the back of his neck. A long, restless night had left him edgy. Irritable. 'Forensics?'

'Waiting on a DNA profile from the hair strand found in the bedroom.'

'Chase it up. Today. Then contact those fools from the *polizia* and check their records for a match.' He drummed his fingers on his desk, cast a brooding look out of the window. 'And the neighbours?'

'One left to interview. Female. In her fifties.'

'Okay. *Bien*. Review that list of artists I emailed to you yesterday and get—' Nico broke off, sat forward, then surged up out of his chair. *What the hell?* 'Bruno, I'll call you back.'

He slammed down the phone, strode through the house and out onto the limestone terrace. Raising a hand to shield his eyes against the midmorning sun, he stared beyond the pool to the cliff's edge—and felt his heart punch into his throat.

He paused, drew a deep breath and loosed his voice on a furious bellow. *'Marietta!'*

She didn't hear him—or chose to ignore him. The latter, most likely. Anger spiked and he spat out a curse.

He veered onto a little-used dirt path that meandered through tall grasses and clusters of wild lavender and rosemary. The wheels of her chair had left tracks in the dirt. Tracks that led directly to the edge of the plunging forty-foot cliff.

'Marietta!' he shouted again, and knew she'd heard him this time because her shoulders flinched. And yet she didn't so much as turn her head.

Another few strides and the pump of adrenaline through his veins gave way to relief. She was sitting farther back from the edge than he'd thought. He reached her side, balled his hands lest he curl them over her slender shoulders and shake her.

'What the *hell* are you doing?'

She looked up, her expression faintly astonished. 'Enjoying the scenery,' she said, her air of calm making his jaw clench.

He jammed his fists in his jeans pockets. 'Is there something wrong with the view from the terrace?'

'Of course not. But I sat on your terrace all day yesterday. I need a change or I'll go mad. Besides…'

She rolled forward and he pulled his hands out of his jeans so fast he heard one of the pockets rip.

'I've been dying to look at the beach down there.'

He stepped in front of her. 'That's far enough.'

She huffed out a breath. 'Seriously, Nico. You're as bad as my brother. What do you think I'm going to do? Push myself over the edge?' She craned her neck to peek around him. 'Are those steps cut into the cliff?'

He ground his molars together. '*Oui.* But they're extremely old. Probably eroded. Unsafe.'

'Probably? You mean…you don't *know*?' Her eyebrows arched. 'As in…you've never been down there before?'

He folded his arms over his chest. 'It's just a beach.'

'But it's *your* beach…and it's a beautiful beach. Why would you not go down there?'

A vein throbbed in his temple. *Mon Dieu*. Had he ever met a woman so infuriating? So unpredictable?

He let his gaze rake over her, from her high glossy ponytail to her sun-kissed shoulders, all the way down to the pink-painted toenails poking out of her strappy white sandals. Her white knee-length shorts left her pale, delicate shins visible and her stretchy pink spaghetti-strap top made her breasts look nothing short of magnificent.

How could a woman look so alluring and be so annoying all at the same time?

He brought his gaze back to her face. Colour flared over those high cheekbones and a pulse flickered at the base of her throat. Their eyes met and hers widened a fraction—and he wondered if she felt it too. That pulse of heat in the air. That pull of attraction.

Belatedly he realised she'd spoken again. 'Pardon?'

'A prisoner,' she repeated, frowning at him. 'I feel like a prisoner, Nico.'

A prisoner.

His gut twisted hard, turning in on itself, and his mind descended instantly to a dark, savage place.

Julia's final, terror-filled days on this earth had been as a prisoner, held captive by the kidnappers who'd extracted a hefty ransom from her father—then left her in a ditch to die.

'Nico?'

Marietta's voice penetrated the sudden thick haze in his head.

'Are you all right?'

He gave himself a mental shake, shoved a lid over that dark, bottomless hole before it sucked him into its destructive vortex. 'I'm trying to keep you safe, Marietta. That's all.'

'I know. But my stalker's in Rome—there's no threat to me here.'

She edged her chair forward until her toes nearly touched his shins. When she tilted her head back the appeal in her huge brown eyes had a profound effect on him.

'Nico… I spent six months of my life in a rehabilitation unit—two of those months flat on my back, staring at the same ceiling and walls, day in, day out. I had no control…no choice… I felt angry and scared and trapped—I guess that's why I get a little stir-crazy when I'm cooped up in one place for too long.'

Guilt coiled inside him. He hadn't considered that the isolation in which he found solace would, for Marietta, feel like captivity.

Silently cursing his thoughtlessness, he dropped to his haunches in front of her. 'Tell me what you'd like to do today.'

Her face broke into a smile and for a second—just a second—Nico felt as if he'd stepped out of the darkness into the light.

CHAPTER SEVEN

'COFFEE TO FINISH?'

Nico's question drew Marietta's attention from the young couple sitting several tables away in the bistro's outdoor courtyard. She looked across the table she and Nico shared, its surface crowded with empty platters and dishes from their delicious seafood lunch. '*Si*. Please.'

A moment later Josephine's son, Luc, came to clear their table and take their coffee order. He was pleasant, relaxed and friendly—like the rest of his family, all of whom Marietta had met upon their arrival at the quaint seaside restaurant.

Nico's presence had drawn the entire Bouchard clan out to greet them—Josephine and her husband Philippe from the kitchen, and her father, Henri, from the cool, shaded interior of the family-run bistro. The old man had smiled broadly and the two men had greeted each other with obvious warmth—surprising Marietta, until she'd reminded herself that people were multi-faceted and Nico was no different.

Until yesterday she would never have guessed he was a widower—a fact that stirred a pang of emotion every time she thought of it.

A burst of laughter from the young couple drew her gaze back to them. Tourists from the mainland, she guessed. The guy was good-looking, his girlfriend pretty—blonde and suntanned, her slender legs long and bare below a short summer skirt. Their faces were flushed, from the sun or maybe from the wine they were drinking, and they looked happy. Carefree. In love.

'I spoke with Bruno this morning.'

She looked at Nico, so big and handsome here in the open-air courtyard, with its colourful potted flowers and its miniature citrus trees in terracotta planters dotted around the tables. Overhead an umbrella shaded them from the sun's brilliance and beyond the broad span of his shoulders the water sparkled in the harbour. She couldn't imagine him looking carefree—not with that constant air of alertness about him—but he did look more at ease than she'd ever seen him before. That rare smile—the one she'd caught her first glimpse of last night—had made a couple of stunning reappearances, and each time it had stopped the breath in her lungs.

'Is there any news?' she asked, wondering why he hadn't mentioned it before now, and yet grateful that he hadn't. For a while over lunch she'd felt like just another tourist, enjoying the island.

'Your ex is in the clear.'

Relief surged, even though she hadn't for a moment suspected Davide. 'So…what now? Are there other leads?'

'A couple.'

She waited for him to elaborate. When he didn't, she suppressed a flutter of annoyance. 'I *am* going back in five days,' she reminded him—because staying on the island beyond Friday and missing Ricci's birthday was still a compromise too far.

Nico remained silent, evoking a frisson of disquiet. But then Luc arrived with their coffee and Josephine came out to ask if they'd enjoyed their meal.

'Bellissimo!' Marietta exclaimed.

Josephine beamed. 'You will come and join us for dinner one evening before you leave, *oui*?'

'Of course,' she said, then, fearing she'd spoken out of turn, cast a quick glance at Nico.

But he simply murmured an assent that had Josephine looking pleased before she bustled back to the kitchen.

Marietta sipped her coffee and noticed the young couple get up to leave. The girl giggled and swayed, and her boyfriend caught her but he too was staggering. Grinning, he tossed some euros on the table and then guided the girl out onto the street towards a parked car—and Marietta's belly clenched with alarm.

She dropped her cup into its saucer, reached across the table and grabbed Nico's arm. 'Stop them,' she said urgently, and pointed with her other hand. 'That couple—about to get into the red car. He's drunk.'

Frowning, Nico glanced over his shoulder and then back at her. 'Are you sure?'

'*Si*. I was watching them.' Panic tightened her grip on his arm. 'Nico, please…'

He stood abruptly and strode out onto the street, calling something to the young man, who already had the driver's door open. An exchange in French followed and the younger man's demeanour morphed from jovial to belligerent—and then outright combative when Nico snatched his key away from him.

Nico, looking remarkably cool for a man who had just dodged a wildly thrown punch, pinned the tourist against the car, and then all of a sudden Luc and his father Philippe were there, helping to defuse the situation.

The tension eased from Marietta's shoulders but an icy chill had gripped her and her hands shook. She curled them tight, closed her eyes for a minute.

'Marietta?'

She looked up. Nico was crouched beside her chair, and she searched over his shoulder for the couple.

'They're inside,' he told her. 'Josephine's encouraging them to stay, to drink some water and coffee, have something to eat.'

She nodded, grateful, and yet still the iciness inside her wouldn't abate. She had been that girl once—young and beautiful, with her whole life ahead of her. If only someone had stopped her and her friends from getting into that car...

She shook her head. Dispelled the thought. She knew better than to dwell on *if only*. She picked up her cup, took a fortifying gulp of coffee, felt relieved when Nico stood. He returned to his chair but then studied her, and her skin heated and prickled despite the chill in her veins.

'You did a good thing.'

'*We* did a good thing,' she corrected.

He shrugged. 'You were the one who noticed them—and you were right. The kid's way over the limit.'

Marietta wrapped her hands around her cup. Stared into the dark brew. 'I couldn't watch them get into that car.'

Nico was silent a moment. 'Your accident?'

She looked up. 'You know about that?'

'Only what your brother told me—that your paralysis resulted from a car crash.'

Her stomach gave a hard, vicious twist. It always did when she recalled her fragmented memories of that night. The mangled wreckage and broken glass. The whimpers of the girl dying beside her. Her own pain and then—worse—no pain at all. Nothing but numbness and fear.

Her grip on her cup tightened. 'I was young and stupid…drinking at a party Leo hadn't wanted me to attend. I knew my friend had had too much to drink when he offered me a ride.' She grimaced. It was never easy to admit your own stupidity. 'I still got into that car.'

'And your friend…?' Nico asked quietly.

'He and the two girls in the car with us died.' She pushed her cup aside, her mouth too bitter suddenly for coffee. 'I was the only survivor.'

'I'm sorry, Marietta.'

Nico's voice was deep and sincere, but she told herself the warmth spreading through her belly was from the coffee, not the effect of that rich, soothing baritone. 'I made a mistake and I live with the consequences of that mistake every day,' she said. 'If I can stop someone else from suffering a similar fate, I will.'

Because no one deserved to suffer what she had. To have their life so drastically altered by one foolish, split-second decision. To have to face up to the bitter realisation that their future was going to be vastly different from the one they'd envisaged. She'd always wanted a career in art, and she'd achieved that, but as a girl she had dreamed of other things, too—love, marriage, children—things she'd eventually had to accept were no longer in her future.

Nico's blue eyes were unfathomable, as always, and suddenly she regretted opening up to him. This man knew so much about her already, and she knew next to nothing about him—especially his past. She'd known he'd served in the French Foreign Legion— that alone was fascinating—but knowing he was a widower... It touched something inside her. Made her want to see beneath that tough, formidable exterior. And yet she couldn't imagine she ever would. Nico guarded his privacy like a fortress—and he'd made it clear two-way sharing wasn't on the agenda.

'Anyway,' she said, 'the accident was a long time ago. I try not to dwell on the past.' She brightened her voice. 'Lunch was lovely. Thank you. Can we go and see the old ruins now?'

His thick brows drew together. 'You really want to see a crumbling pile of ancient stones?'

'I thought we were doing what *I* want to do today?'

His eyes narrowed. 'You are a stubborn woman, Marietta Vincenti.'

She raised her chin. 'So I've been told.'

Nico stepped onto the terrace with a bottle and two glasses in his hands and a strong sense of *déjà vu*.

Tonight, however, the bottle was an expensive Burgundy rather than cognac, and the mood in the air—if not entirely tension-free—was an improvement on yesterday.

He couldn't remember the last time he'd spent almost an entire day with one woman. Marietta was beautiful and he couldn't deny she made his blood heat, but she also fascinated him on a level most women didn't. She was strong. A woman who'd fought her way back from a major life-altering trauma—*a survivor.*

She was different from the women whose company he normally sought and that was the attraction, he assured himself. Nothing more.

And he couldn't deny that today had been…pleasurable.

She had charmed the entire Bouchard clan, including old Henri, and though the incident with the young couple had seemed to shake her she'd bounced back—enough to demand he take her to see the old fortress.

Her fascination with the ruins had bemused Nico. The ancient stronghold that had once defended the island against marauding pirates was, to his eye, no more than a dull, crumbling edifice, and yet Marietta had taken the time to snap photos from every vantage point her wheelchair had allowed her to reach.

Then she had asked him to piggyback her up the spiral staircase of the stone tower to see the view.

It had been torture. Sweet, exquisite torture.

Those soft, lush breasts pressed into his back. Her slender arms looped around his neck. Her warm breath misting over his nape.

He had thought that lifting her into and out of his Jeep throughout the day had tested his control. Carrying her on his back, all that feminine warmth and vanilla and strawberry scent enveloping him, had been a hundred times more challenging.

She was wheeling out of the house now, a platter of cheeses, olives and cured meats expertly balanced on her lap. A bread basket filled with the fresh mini-baguettes Josephine had given them this afternoon already sat on the table.

A minute later she was piling thick slices of cheese into a baguette. 'I shouldn't be hungry after our enormous lunch,' she said. 'It must be all the sea air.'

Nico watched her bite into the baguette. He liked it that she wasn't overly dainty in the way she ate. She tackled her food with enthusiasm. Appreciation. A sign of her Italian heritage, perhaps?

'The air quality here is pristine,' he said. 'I crave it when I've been in Paris or New York or any major city for too long.'

She swallowed. 'Do you have homes in Paris and New York?'

'Apartments.'

She nodded—as if that didn't surprise her. Her head tilted to one side. 'So, what does a man who runs a multi-billion-dollar global security company do with his time off?'

He fingered the stem of his glass. Tried not to notice how her mouth wrapped around the end of her baguette. 'That depends,' he said finally.

'On what?'

'On what kind of recreation I'm in the mood for.'

He enjoyed the sudden bloom of pink in her cheeks more than he should have.

Her gaze thinned. 'Holidays,' she said. 'Where do you go on holiday?'

'I don't.'

She frowned. 'You don't take holidays?'

'This is where I come to unwind.'

'Alone?'

'Oui,' he said. 'Alone.'

Her eyes widened. 'So you don't bring your... friends here?'

He lifted an eyebrow. 'Do you mean to ask me if I bring my lovers here, Marietta?'

The colour in her cheeks brightened. She picked up her wine glass, took a large sip and sat back. 'Do you not get lonely here on your own?'

He shrugged. 'I like the quiet.' Which wasn't strictly true. He craved the isolation more than the quiet itself. The disconnection from the world and the people in it.

Marietta looked towards the ocean and the setting sun. Half a dozen shades of orange and gold—colours she would no doubt give fancy names to—streaked the sky. 'It *is* peaceful here. And beautiful.' Her gaze returned to his. 'Are there no other places you'd like to visit, though? Things you'd like to see?'

He shifted in his chair. 'I've seen more things in

this world than you can imagine,' he said. 'And most of them I never wish to see again.'

He heard something dark and bleak in his own voice then. Marietta studied him, and he shrugged off the notion that she could somehow see the darkness inside him…the *emptiness* he'd never been able to fill since losing his wife.

'Well,' she said, 'I haven't seen enough of the world. There's plenty of places I'd like to see…things I'd like to do.'

'Such as…?'

'The pyramids in Egypt.'

His brows dropped. *Was she kidding?* 'Do you have any idea how volatile that region is?'

She lifted her shoulders. 'Isn't the whole world "volatile" these days?'

'Oui. Which is why travellers need to be more selective about the destinations they choose. More safety conscious.'

'I agree. But no one can live in a protective bubble, can they? If people did they'd never go anywhere, never do anything. Living involves risk, whether we like it or not.'

'Risk can be minimised through sensible choices.'

Marietta sighed. 'You sound like my brother.'

'That's because Leo is a smart man,' he clipped out.

She flicked her hair over one shoulder. She wore another halterneck top tonight, this one red and floaty and partially see-through. Nico kept his gaze above her collarbone.

'None of that diminishes my desire to see the pyramids,' she said. 'In fact it doesn't change anything on my wish list.'

His brows sank lower. 'You have a *list*?'

'*Si.*'

'Tell me about it.'

Her chin notched up a fraction. 'I'm not sure I want to.'

'Tell me,' he commanded.

Something flashed across her face. Annoyance, he guessed. She took a slow sip of her wine, fuelling his impatience.

'Okay—I want to do a tandem skydive.'

Mon Dieu.

'No.'

The word shot from his mouth of its own volition.

Her eyebrows rose. 'I don't need anyone's *permission*, Nico.'

His jaw tightened. 'It's dangerous.'

'So is getting into a car and driving on the *autostrada*,' she said, and the significance of that statement didn't escape him. 'Besides...' She flung a hand in his direction. 'I bet *you've* jumped out of a plane plenty of times. Don't elite soldiers do that sort of thing?'

The reference to his soldiering days gave Nico only brief pause. His service in the French Foreign

Legion was no secret. The Legion's flame-like emblem and motto—*Honneur et Fidélité*—were inked on his upper left arm and had been for eighteen years. He had knocked on the Legion's door—literally, because that was the only way to gain entry—on the day of his eighteenth birthday, gone on to serve his five contracted years, and then got the hell out.

No doubt he'd mentioned his service to her brother at some point, though Nico never spoke of those years in any detail. Trekking through humid, insect-ridden jungles and dry, shelterless deserts, defending himself and his unit against lethal attacks from rebel forces and random insurgents, policing war zones where their allies had been indistinguishable from their enemies and they hadn't known who to trust—none of it made for idle conversation.

Still, those five years had put into perspective the many childhood injustices he'd suffered as a ward of the French state—had made them seem almost trivial. Insignificant. And, yes, during his time as a legionnaire—and as a military contractor—he'd jumped out of a few planes.

'Irrelevant, Marietta. What else is on your list?'

She sipped her wine, took her time again. 'A hot air balloon ride. Let me guess,' she added. 'That's dangerous, too.'

'You think floating two thousand feet above the ground in an oversized picnic basket is *safe*?'

She rolled her eyes. 'This from the man who flies a helicopter?'

He scowled. No comparison. His chopper was a solid machine, designed and built by aeronautical specialists to exacting safety standards. A hot air balloon was nothing but yards of silk filled with...*hot air*. It would be a frosty day in hell when he climbed into one of those things.

'Is there anything remotely sensible on your list?'

Her lips curved, as if she were actually enjoying this conversation. 'Sensible isn't any fun, is it? But, yes—there are things you'd probably consider low-risk.'

'Like?'

'Swimming in the ocean...' That little smile continued to play about her mouth. 'Naked.'

And just like that, the steady, persistent hum of awareness in his blood intensified—until he felt as if a high-voltage current arced through his veins.

'Somewhere private, of course,' she said, and then her eyes widened as if she'd had an enlightening thought. 'Your beach would be perfect!'

All at once an image of Marietta floating naked in the clear seawater at the foot of his cliff flashed into his head. Heat and lust ignited in his belly, along with the certain knowledge that she *did* feel the same pull of attraction he did. He could see it—in the sudden hectic colour in her cheeks. In the way her eyes glittered and held his in silent challenge.

She was provoking him.

Playing with fire.

He lunged up out of his chair, strode to her side and seized her chin. The dark look he gave her should have subdued and intimidated. Instead her lips parted, soft and inviting, as though she were anticipating…a *kiss*.

Dieu.

He *wanted* to kiss her. Wanted to crush his mouth onto hers and let her feel the full, unleashed power of the lust she was deliberately inciting. Wanted to punish her for dangling temptation in front of him like an enticing treat he didn't deserve.

He held himself rigid. Controlled. 'Be *very* careful what you wish for, Marietta.'

And then he released her and stalked into the house, back to his study—where he should have stayed in the first place.

Nico stood near the edge of the vertiginous cliff and stared down at the small crescent-shaped beach he had never set foot upon.

On this side of the island the coastline was rocky, precipitous in places, but here and there the cliffs formed inlets with sandy sheltered beaches and calm channels of crystal blue water ideal for swimming.

Yesterday he had told Marietta the steps carved into the ancient rock face might be eroded, but in truth they appeared sturdy—probably as safe now as

they had been a century ago. Until this morning he'd
never thought about using them. Had never given the
beach more than a passing thought.

Had he been in a war zone, he'd have cast his
trained soldier's eye over the isolated cove and
deemed it a death trap—the perfect location to fall
prey to ambush—but he wasn't a soldier any longer
and the island wasn't a war zone.

And he wasn't standing here right now thinking
about danger hotspots and military manoeuvres.

He was thinking about the woman he had wanted
to kiss last night and her damned wish list. About
the sand down there on his beach and whether it was
coarse or soft. About the temperature of the water—
and Marietta's skin… How she would feel pressed
against him if they swam together naked.

Ridiculous, *insane* thoughts.

Thoughts he would not normally entertain.

But, by God, she'd got under his skin. Ignited a
hunger that hadn't relinquished its grip but rather had
burned hotter, fiercer, during the night.

Did she understand what kind of man she was
toying with? What sex with him would mean and—
more importantly—what it *wouldn't* mean?

He jammed his hands into his jeans pockets.

He was not a tender, romantic man. He was an
ex-soldier with a grisly past. A man who had loved
and lost and vowed he would never again tumble into
that soul-destroying abyss. His liaisons with women

served one rudimentary purpose, and for that reason he chose experienced women. Never innocents.

And yet Marietta was no ingénue. She was smart and confident. Strong and resilient. A woman who didn't fear the world, who understood what it meant to accept the consequences of her actions. *A woman who knew what she wanted*.

Did she want *him*?

He closed his eyes, searched the dark, twisted labyrinth of his conscience. Which would make him the better man? Indulging her? Or keeping his distance?

He opened his eyes and studied the ancient steps.

Were they as solid as they appeared?

He pulled his hands from his pockets and moved closer to the cliff's edge. *Only one way to find out.*

CHAPTER EIGHT

MARIETTA CLUNG TO Nico's back as he paused at the top of the cliff, her belly a cauldron of excitement and nerves. She couldn't believe they were doing this.

She peered over his shoulder, all the way down to the crescent-shaped strip of white sand at the foot of the cliff. It was a very, *very* long way down, and the steps hewn into the rock face were much steeper than she'd imagined. Her arms tightened reflexively around his neck.

'I've got you, *chérie.*'

His deep voice seemed to resonate through her chest, and the unexpected endearment made her pulse hitch.

'Ready?' he said.

'Yes.'

As ready as I'll ever be.

And then he started down the steps and the buzz of anticipation turned into a wild flutter. They *were* doing this. And she really couldn't believe it. Not after last night, when he'd stormed off and she'd been certain she had pushed him too far.

She'd sat by the pool, watching the rich golds and ambers and deep purples of the sunset bleed into one another, and tried to attribute her uncharacteristic behaviour to having had too much sun during the day. Too much wine with her supper.

But neither of those excuses was valid.

The truth was she had wanted to provoke him— because a reckless yearning had been building in her all day. A yearning to find out if a man like Nico could be attracted to a woman like her—a woman whom society largely viewed as *disabled*.

She knew the wheelchair frightened most men. Some wrongly assumed she couldn't have sex or wouldn't enjoy it. Others, she guessed, were repelled by her useless legs. Davide had been different in that regard, and their sex-life had been healthy, satisfying—though not the kind of passionate, all-consuming sex she'd fantasised about as a teenager.

She had a feeling deep in her belly, where the butterflies had gathered *en masse* now, that sex with Nico would be the kind of wild, passionate sex she'd long ago resigned herself to never experiencing.

And Nico *was* attracted to her. She had seen the evidence as soon as she'd made that provocative suggestion about swimming naked at his beach. Had seen it stamped on his face—a raw hunger her body

had instinctively responded to with its own powerful throb of need.

He had almost kissed her. Standing there grasp-
ing her chin and glaring down at her, anger and desire pulsing off him in waves, he had looked like a
man fighting for control.

And, oh, she had *wanted* him to kiss her. Even
knowing that if he did it wouldn't be gentle. That
there would be fire and fury behind his kiss. When
he hadn't—when he'd walked away from her instead—her disappointment had been so intense it
had felt like a physical blow against her ribs.

He'd negotiated the last few steps now, and Marietta's eyes widened as he carried her across the sand
to where a blue-and-white-striped awning stood in a
sheltered lee off the cliff. Beneath the awning lay a
picnic rug and a bunch of big, comfy-looking cushions, and on a corner of the rug, shaded from the direct heat of the midday sun, sat a large wicker basket.

'Nico!' Her voice came out breathless. 'How many
trips did this take you?'

'A few.'

He knelt on the rug and she slid off his back,
the friction between their bodies teasing her already
over-sensitised nipples into hard, aching nubs. She
plucked her tee shirt away from her breasts before
he turned, glad that she'd put the loose-fitting white
tee on over her yellow bikini top. She slipped her

hands under her legs and straightened them out in front of her.

Nico propped two cushions behind her back. 'Comfortable?'

She nodded, looked around her. 'It's beautiful, Nico.'

She ran her hand through the warm sand. The pearly-white granules felt luxuriously soft as they sifted through her fingers. She looked towards the calm water in the inlet. It was a clear, stunning turquoise—the kind seen on postcards of exotic locales that most people only ever dreamed of visiting. Best of all, the cove was utterly, totally private.

'I can't believe you've never been down here before.'

Nico shrugged and kicked off his sneakers. He wore khaki shorts and a black polo shirt and he looked big and vital and masculine. He lifted the lid off the hamper. 'I didn't know what you'd want to eat…' He started pulling out items. 'So I brought a bit of everything.'

He wasn't joking. There were fruits, olives, crackers, breads, pickles and a variety of meats and cheeses in a small cooler, plus water, soda and two bottles of wine—a red Cabernet and a chilled white. Cutlery, plastic plates and glasses emerged as well, along with condiments and a packet of paper serviettes.

Marietta couldn't help but laugh. 'I bet you never go anywhere unprepared.'

Nico opened a water bottle and handed it to her. 'Who's the guy you want to be with when disaster strikes?'

She rolled her eyes. 'You,' she conceded.

A smug look crossed his face. He planted his hands on his thighs and surveyed the enormous spread of food. 'I hope you're hungry.'

'Not *this* hungry.' She reached for a bunch of green grapes and smiled. 'But I'll give it my best shot.'

In the end, however, Marietta found she could eat very little. Thoughts of what they might do together after lunch made her stomach too jittery. She did manage a small glass of white wine, hoping it would lend her some much needed Dutch courage.

Now she lay on her back under the awning, her eyes closed, wondering if she needn't have bothered with the wine. If perhaps she'd been a fool to think anything was going to happen beyond a picnic lunch on the beach. Because Nico hadn't suggested they swim, nor made a move to touch her, nor even so much as uttered a word in the last fifteen minutes.

Yet a definite tension permeated the air. Her sixth sense could intuit it—just as her other senses could detect *him*. The scent of soap and the faint tang of clean, male sweat. The sound of his breathing, deep and even. And his *heat*. She could feel the heat that seemed always to radiate from him, as if his body were a non-stop furnace. Whenever he was close that heat enveloped her, penetrating her skin, sinking into her bones and making her feel as if she were melting.

She opened her eyes and turned her head to look at him. He lay beside her, his eyes closed, but she knew he wasn't sleeping. Nico didn't strike her as the kind of man who indulged in daytime naps. In fact she half suspected that even at night he slept with one eye open. She let her gaze drift down, away from his strong profile, and mentally braced herself for the heart-stopping impact of his bare torso.

He was utter perfection. Hard muscle, smooth skin, dark, crisp hair in all the places a man should have hair—including a liberal sprinkling over his sculpted pecs and a narrow line bisecting his washboard abs. A black ink tattoo adorned his upper left arm and a long rough-edged scar curled over the same shoulder.

I've seen more things in this world than you can imagine—and most of them I never wish to see again.

His words from the previous evening came back to her, sending a shiver through her now as they had then. Nico had sounded so grim in that moment, so haunted, and she'd wanted to ask him what he'd seen that had been so terrible he never wanted to see it again. That had made him into a man who guarded his privacy and kept himself aloof from the world. But she had reined in her curiosity, knowing it wouldn't be welcome. Knowing instinctively that if she probed, their conversation would be over before it started.

Her gaze trailed the jagged line of the scar, and she recognised the tattoo on his arm as the emblem of the French Foreign Legion. Had the awful things he'd seen been the horrors of war? Of course. They must have been. Soldiers who served in conflict zones witnessed first-hand the worst of mankind's atrocities.

'Why did you join the Legion?'

She grimaced as soon as the words were out of her mouth. She hadn't meant to speak them aloud. She opened her mouth to retract the question—but he spoke first.

'Because I was eighteen and full of testosterone and didn't know what else to do with my life.'

Nico kept his eyes closed as he spoke. He'd surprised himself by answering her question. Normally he shut down conversations that ventured too far into personal territory, but right then he figured talking was the lesser of two evils. The greater evil—the dark, sexual desire prowling through him—couldn't be unleashed. Not on Marietta.

He realised that now.

Belatedly.

Hell. What had he been thinking? She wasn't one of the easy, vacuous, forgettable women with whom he occasionally hooked up for the sole purpose of satisfying his physical needs. She was Marietta, his friend's sister—a woman he respected. A woman who was *un*forgettable.

He had told himself she was no ingénue, and she wasn't. No innocent would have goaded him last night without understanding where such provocation could lead. What she was *inviting*. And yet as they'd sat there on the sand, sharing food and idle small talk—the kind of simple pleasure his late wife would have loved—he'd looked at Marietta and thought about the incident at the bistro, her concern for the young couple. And he'd realised that after everything this woman had been through, she was still pure. She still had compassion in her heart. Still cared about others.

How could he touch her and not taint her with his darkness? He had nothing to give her. Nothing to offer beyond the pleasures of the flesh.

'Did your parents not object?'

He slid his right hand under the back of his head and continued to keep his eyes closed. She'd taken her tee shirt off after they'd eaten, and seeing her in that yellow bikini top only inflamed his libido.

'I didn't have parents,' he said.

'Oh… I… I'm sorry, Nico.' She fell silent a moment. 'Did you lose them when you were young?'

'My mother died of a stroke when I was six,' he said, surprising himself yet again. He couldn't remember the last time he'd spoken of his childhood. Couldn't remember the last time someone had shown an interest, aside from Julia. 'She was a solo parent—I never knew my father.'

He heard Marietta shift, felt the weight of her gaze on him.

'Did you live with relatives after your mother passed away?'

'My mother didn't have any relatives. I became a ward of the state and spent the remainder of my childhood in children's homes and foster care.'

'Oh, Nico… That must have been difficult.'

It hadn't been a walk in the park. His mother had been a good woman, a loving *maman*, and he'd missed her. But he'd survived. Years of being shuffled around in an indifferent welfare system had thickened his skin.

'Don't go all sympathetic on me, Marietta. Every second person out there has had a difficult childhood.' He opened his eyes, turned his head to look at her. 'I understand you and Leo lost your mother young—and your father a few years later?'

'*Si*. And I missed my mother desperately—which is probably why I acted out as a teenager. But Leo and I had each other. You…' Her voice grew husky. 'You had no one.'

And he hadn't needed anyone. Certainly hadn't wanted to get close to anyone. *Why bother?* he'd thought as a boy. *Why attach yourself to someone just so they could leave you or die.*

It was a pity he hadn't remembered that lesson

before he'd married Julia. Instead he'd let life teach it to him all over again—only much more brutally the second time around.

He shrugged, looked up at the awning shielding them from the sun. 'There are worse things in life than being alone.'

'Like going to war?' She touched him then, trailing the tip of one finger over his scar. 'Did you get this when you were in the Legion?'

He sat up, forcing her hand to fall away. *'Oui.'*

'How?'

Mon Dieu. Did her curiosity know no limits?

'It's a shrapnel wound,' he told her, because maybe if he shared something ugly with her she'd see the damaged man he was and realise she didn't want him. Not the way she thought she did.

'From an explosion?'

'A suicide bomber.' He twisted his head around to see her face. 'A twelve-year-old boy.'

'Mio Dio...' she breathed, her expression horrified. 'That's awful.'

'That's the modern face of war.' He kept his voice hard, unaffected, *emotionless*. Because that was what he'd learned to do as a soldier. Control his emotions, follow orders, focus on the job and divide those he encountered into one of two camps—ally or enemy. Except that last part hadn't always been easy.

Marietta pressed her palm against his bare back, the contact so unexpected he nearly flinched.

'I'm so sorry for all the terrible things you must have seen, Nico,' she said, in that soft, sympathetic voice that seemed to curl around him, *through* him.

Her hand moved, stroking over his skin, setting fire to a host of nerve-endings which all led like a series of lit fuses to one place. *His groin.*

'Marietta,' he growled, 'what are you doing?'

Marietta wasn't sure she knew the answer to that question. She only knew that she'd felt compelled to reach out in some way, and that once she'd touched him—once she'd made contact with all that smooth, hot skin and sculpted muscle—she hadn't been able to draw her hand away. Hadn't *wanted* to.

He moved with lightning speed. Before she understood his intent he was leaning over her, one hand clamped around her wrist, imprisoning her hand above her head. His expression was dark. Almost angry.

Her heart thumped in her chest.

'You don't want this, Marietta.'

'Want what?' she whispered—but she knew what he meant. Of course she did. She wasn't naive. He hadn't carried her all the way down here just to have lunch on the beach.

But something had changed since they'd got here. Something had caused him to withdraw, have second thoughts.

It felt like a rejection—and it stung.

'Not what—*who*,' he said harshly. 'You don't want *me*, Marietta.'

She pushed up her chin, feeling reckless and bold. Angry even. How *dared* he tell her what she didn't want? 'Why?'

He breathed hard, his nostrils flaring. 'I'm not the kind of man you want to get close to.'

'Why?' she challenged again, her blood thundering in her ears now. 'Because you've seen some terrible things? *Experienced* some terrible things? Things you don't think I could possibly understand?' She struggled to free her wrist. 'Let me go, Nico,' she demanded.

He did, and she levered herself upright, forcing him back from her. 'Do you think you're the only one with scars?' She leaned forward over her legs, exposing her back. 'The one under my left shoulder blade is from the accident,' she told him. 'The rest are from surgeries—*failed* surgeries—and every one of them represents a shattered hope. A shattered dream.'

She dropped back to her elbows, locked her gaze with his.

'I lay in the wreckage of that car for thirty minutes, with two dead friends and another friend dying beside me, before the emergency services arrived.' She hiked up her chin, swallowed down hard on the lump in her throat. 'I haven't been to war, Nico. I haven't seen or done the things you have. But I *do* know something about death and survival.'

Her blood continued to pound, flushing her skin, making the pulse in her throat leap. The after-effects of the wine combined with her anger and the sight of all that potent, half-naked masculinity before her spurred her on to more recklessness.

She reached out and laid her palm against his chest, her fingers nestling in the fine covering of crisp hairs. 'Maybe I *don't* know what kind of man is hidden away in here. But whoever he is—whoever you *think* he is—he doesn't scare me.'

Deliberately she glided the tip of her little finger over his nipple and heard the sudden sharp hiss of his indrawn breath. But his big body remained taut and rigid, unmoving except for the powerful rise and fall of his chest beneath her hand. She searched his face, looking for signs of desire—for the flash of hunger she'd seen there last night—but the seconds stretched and nothing happened.

The flush receded from her skin and her insides turned cold and then hot again with a horrible, humiliating thought.

She snatched her hand back.

Dio. Had she read this all wrong? Had she imagined something that wasn't really there?

The moment seemed to click into slow motion. Nico's eyes narrowed, his mouth opening as if he was about to speak. But she gave her head a violent shake and fell back onto the cushions, squeezing her eyes closed. She couldn't look at him. He was too perfect. A man like him could have any woman in the world. Why would he take *her*? Unless…

Her face burned. *Stupid, stupid…*

'I think you're right.' She forced the words out between stiff lips. 'I *don't* want this.' Pride made her voice brittle. Defensive. 'I don't need pity sex.'

A sound came from above her—a harsh, ferocious growl of a sound—and she snapped her eyes open.

Nico grasped her wrist, not gently, and pulled her hand to his groin.

'You think *this* is pity?'

A gasp caught in her throat. Nico's eyes blazed into hers, but it wasn't the glittering anger and raw desire she saw that stripped her lungs of air—it was the irrefutable evidence of his arousal, big and thick and rock-hard against her hand. Heat coiled in her belly, and she curled her fingers around his impressive length. *Santo cielo.* He was enormous—and hard. For *her*.

A low, guttural curse shot from his mouth. 'Marietta—' The way he rasped her name was half-warning, half-groan. 'I want you,' he said roughly, tightening his fingers around her wrist, thrusting his groin harder into her hand to encourage her grip. 'Make no mistake about that. But you need to be certain this is what you want—because believe me when I say *this* is the point of no return.'

The fierce heat in his gaze, the solid, rigid length of him in her hand, extinguished her doubts. She squeezed him, giving her answer, and he pulled her hand away from him and loomed above her. Anticipation shivered through her and then his mouth covered hers, and that sudden, shocking clash of lips was ten times more electrifying than she could ever have imagined.

The world spun and she reached blindly for an anchor, until her hands latched on to the hot, hard flesh of his shoulders. He moved and she tightened her grip on him, terrified he was going to end the kiss, but he simply angled his head so he could take it deeper. His tongue stroked over her lips, then thrust between them—and the explosion of heat and earthiness in her mouth was unlike anything she'd ever experienced.

When he raised his head colour slashed his cheekbones, emphasising their prominence, and his eyes had darkened to an inky blue. His gaze raked over her face and lower, down to her breasts in the revealing yellow bikini. He fingered the gold clasp holding the triangles of fabric together and then, with a single flick, unfastened the top. The fabric fell away, exposing her to his scrutiny.

'Spectaculaire...' he murmured, and cupped his hand around her right breast.

Her shoulder blades arched off the cushion, her body straining instinctively into his touch. When his thumb stroked over her extended nipple the sensation was exquisite, but nowhere close to being enough. She needed *more*...

She moaned. 'Nico...'

A dark, anticipatory gleam lit his eyes. He lowered his head and sucked her nipple into his mouth, gently at first and then, when she gasped and drove her hands into his hair, harder, using his tongue and his teeth to tease and torment, until she cried out some incoherent words, which he obviously took as encouragement, because he popped her nipple out of his mouth and lavished the same attention on her left one.

Her nails scraped over his scalp. '*Dio*... Nico...'

Something broke loose inside her. Something wild. Demanding. She thrust her chest upwards, urging him on until she was conscious of nothing else besides the heat of his mouth and his tongue and the tight, coiling sensation inside her. Time stopped, ceased to exist, and she didn't know if seconds or minutes had passed when she registered the faint metallic slide of a zipper—realised Nico's hand was at the front of her shorts.

She froze. Only for a moment, but he felt it. His mouth slipped off her nipple, and she wanted to groan.

'I'm not changing my mind,' she said hurriedly, cursing the insecurity that had struck her out of the blue.

She tried pulling his head back down, but he resisted.

He cupped her jaw. 'You froze. Why?'

Inexplicably, her hands trembled. She let go of him and curled them against her stomach, closed her eyes.

'Marietta—'

'My legs,' she whispered. 'They're not...' *Not beautiful.* Her face heated.

'Open your eyes.'

She did, and they prickled dangerously. *Madre di Dio.* What was wrong with her? She *wanted* this. He wanted *her.* Why was she suddenly afraid of revealing her body to him?

'You are beautiful, Marietta,' he said. 'And I want *all* of you.' His hand tightened on her jaw when she would have looked away. 'Do you understand me?'

She stared at him, and then she swallowed and nodded. He dropped a scorching kiss on her mouth. Then he pushed to his feet, removed his shorts and briefs and stood before her fully naked.

The moisture evaporated inside her mouth. Her imagination had not done him justice. He was glorious, every part of him lean and muscled. Her gaze trailed from his broad chest down over the ridges of his abdomen and lower, to where his arousal jutted proudly from the nest of dark hair at the juncture of his thighs. Her belly turned molten. He was so hard. So *big.*

He dropped to his knees, slid the zipper the rest of the way down and removed her shorts and bikini bottoms. Heart pounding, she shrugged off the straps of her bikini top. And then he scooped her into his arms, stood, and carried her across the hot sand into the water.

Kissing, touching, exploring Marietta while immersed in the tepid sea water was the most erotic build-up to sex Nico had ever experienced.

He'd fooled around in water before—taken a woman against the side of a pool more than once—but this...

This was different.

Or maybe it was simply that he was wound so impossibly tight with need for her that he felt as if he might explode at any moment?

God help him.

He hadn't even buried himself inside her yet.

He gave a low, tortured groan, reached between their bodies and pried her fingers from his hard, engorged length before he embarrassed himself and came in the water.

The action earned him a small, petulant frown, but when she reached under the surface, he again seized her wrist.

'*Chérie,*' he growled, 'it will be over before it starts if you keep doing that.'

Her smile was playful, naughty, dialling up the heat in his blood and at the same time reinforcing his sense of relief.

This was the Marietta he knew.

Confident. Spirited. *Pushy*.

The way she'd challenged him on the beach—her boldness, the things she'd said, even her scars—had made him want her even more, until resisting his desire, resisting *hers*, had been impossible. And yet the woman who had frozen beneath him had been vulnerable, insecure—a version of Marietta he hadn't seen before—and his chest had ached with a fierce need to reassure her. To chase the uncertainty from her eyes and bring *this* woman—the one who fired his blood, who challenged him at every turn—back to him.

She wound her arms around his neck now, clinging to him like a silken-skinned mermaid, pressing her lush, caramel-tipped breasts against his chest. He had sucked on those responsive nipples at every opportunity, enjoying her gasps of pleasure as he'd coaxed them into tight, sensitive nubs.

They were ten metres or so from the shore, the water chest-deep, and his feet on the seabed prevented them from drifting.

He kissed her, savouring the warm, salty taste of her mouth and the erotic playfulness of her tongue as it dived between his lips and then retreated, duelling with his.

After a minute he pulled back. Despite his previous claim about the point of no return, he needed to make certain she understood what this was—and *wasn't.* To offer her one last chance to change her mind. Even though it would kill him if she did.

'This is all I can give you,' he said. 'These few days—'

Her fingers landed across his lips. 'I'm not looking for anything more,' she said. 'Here and now—this is all I want...'

And with that the final barrier fell. He dropped an open-mouthed kiss onto the wet, satiny skin between her neck and shoulder and slid his hand under the water, seeking out the silky curls and the velvety V of flesh he'd briefly explored once already—and planned to do so more thoroughly now.

'Tell me where it feels good,' he urged, eager to learn her pleasure points. To understand where she had sensation and where she didn't. He slid his fingers along the seam of delicate flesh, parting, probing, locating the precise spot that made her throw her head back and arch those magnificent breasts against him.

'Oh, *Dio*... There, Nico... *There*...'

He hoisted her higher in the water and clamped his mouth over her nipple, sucking hard while increasing the pressure and movement of his fingers. Her nails sank into his back and the sound she made as she came—something between a purr and a little feminine roar—was the sexiest damn thing he'd ever heard. His body throbbed urgently, almost painfully in response. She dropped her head onto his shoul-

der, her body going limp in his arms, and cursed in
Italian.

Satisfaction rocked through him. 'Was that on
your wish list, *chérie*?'

'No…' she mumbled into his neck. 'But I think I'll
add it, just so that we can do it again and cross it off.'

'I have some other ideas for your list.'

She lifted her head, her dark eyes slumberous.
'Tell me.'

Nico shook his head, shifted her onto his back
and started towards the shore. 'I'm going to show
you instead.'

CHAPTER NINE

MARIETTA HAD EXPECTED Nico to lay her down on the cushions beneath the awning and take her right there on the beach—and she'd have been lying if she'd said a part of her hadn't wanted him to. But he had muttered something about sandy blankets and comfort and now they were in his bedroom—a huge room characterised by clean lines and simple masculine decor—lying naked on soft cotton sheets in a bed so enormous it could have slept an entire family.

Her insides were still molten from the orgasm she'd had in the ocean. She had never climaxed like that before—so easily, so *quickly*. With Davide—and on the occasions when she'd experimented by herself—she'd needed a lot more stimulation. But Nico had brought her to her peak with such little effort it had been almost embarrassing.

She stared at him now, unashamedly, her gaze trailing the length of his powerful body as he lay on his side, stretched out beside her. His arousal was just as proud and fierce as it had been in the water, when she'd wanted so desperately to touch him, and it nudged her hip now, so thick and long she wondered a little nervously if she'd be able to accommodate him.

He drew a fingertip over her belly. 'Comfortable?'

Frustration spiralled. She *was* comfortable, lying on her back, one arm thrown above her head, soft pillows plumped under her shoulders for support. But she didn't *want* to feel comfortable. She didn't want Nico to be solicitous—to treat her like a china doll that might break in two if he was too rough with her. She wanted to feel hot and sweaty and breathless. Wanted to feel his weight on top of her, crushing her into the bed as he drove into the hollow place inside her begging to be filled.

His fingertip traced around her belly button and then her nipples, trailing circles of fire over her skin.

'Is there anything I should know?' he said, his voice rough—as though he wasn't quite as in control of himself as he appeared. 'Anything I can do to make it better for you?'

Her thoughts veered towards the tiny niggle of nervous concern at the back of her mind. Heat surged into her face, and his eyes narrowed.

He gripped her chin. 'What?'.

She swallowed. 'I used to sometimes have issues with—' she closed her eyes, her cheeks burning like hotplates '—with lubrication.'

Silence followed. She cracked her eyes open, expecting to see an awkward look—maybe even disappointment—on Nico's face. Instead his blue eyes glittered with something like…*determination*. As if she had tossed down a gauntlet and he was accepting the challenge. Slowly he rose to his hands and knees.

'Are you worried I won't be able to make you wet for me, *chérie*?'

Her eyes widened. 'No! It's not that… It's just—'

Her eyes grew rounder still as he straddled her, placed his large hands on her skinny thighs and spread them apart.

When he dropped to his stomach, his intent obvious, she babbled again. 'It's not you… It's just that… My body—*oh!*'

Suddenly his mouth was on her—*there*—and the powerful jolt of sensation forced her head back onto the pillow. She caught her breath, clawed her fingers into the sheet beneath her. His mouth was so hot, and his tongue…

Santo cielo!

His tongue was running over and over the spot where her nerve-endings were still very much intact. And then his finger was gently seeking entry, stroking, massaging, sliding deep into…*wetness*. She felt the sweet burn within, the build-up of tension that teased with the promise of a shattering release. Moments later the pressure reached its zenith and she cried out, silence impossible as she split into shards of white light that beamed her skywards and kept her suspended there for a weightless, timeless moment before casting her back to earth.

The bed moved, and she forced open heavy eyelids. Nico was braced above her, his gaze hot. *Satisfied.*

'It's wet down there, *ma petite sirène.*' He kissed her, thrusting his tongue into her mouth, letting her taste herself. '*Very* wet,' he added, and reached over to the nightstand for a condom.

Soon he was sheathed, poised between her legs. He slid his mouth over hers, kissing her long and deep. He lifted his head, his expression as he stared down at her stark. Intense.

'I can't hold back,' he warned, his voice ragged. 'I can't be gentle with you.'

She thrilled to those words. She didn't want gentle—she wanted wild. *Passionate.* She scraped her fingernails down his back and dug them into his firm buttocks.

'Don't be,' she said boldly.

And then he pushed inside her and her mouth slackened on a gasp of pleasure. In one long, powerful thrust he filled her up, and when he started to move, sliding out and thrusting in, again and again, she had no trouble feeling him.

She knew a moment's regret because she couldn't wrap her legs around him, couldn't flex her hips to meet his powerful thrusts. But Nico didn't seem to care; when she looked at him she saw only lust and fierce pleasure carved into his stark features.

He went taut above her, and a second later he shuddered and groaned, signalling his release, and then he was collapsing onto her, pressing his face into her neck.

Marietta wrapped her arms around him and smiled to herself. The weight of his body crushing her into the mattress was, she decided, the most delicious feeling in the world.

Nico awoke from an unusually dreamless sleep, and as he hovered in that place between oblivion and wakefulness he was aware of an unfamiliar sense of…contentment.

He turned onto his side and blinked.

Sunlight streamed through the massive bedroom window and he guessed from the angle that it was late morning—long past the time he would normally rise. He wouldn't normally leave the blinds up either, but last night Marietta had wanted to lie in bed and watch the sunset and he'd indulged her, spooning against her as he'd listened to her *ooh* and *aah* over the fiery sky until his body had stirred and he'd given her something much more impressive to *ooh* and *aah* about.

When the sky had finally turned a deep navy blue and the stars had begun to wink he had turned her onto her back and taken her again, watching her moonlit face as she climaxed before giving in to his own mind-shattering release.

He watched her now, asleep beside him, the sheet rumpled around her waist and her breasts bare. Her ebony eyelashes were dark against her skin, her long mahogany hair fanned out in thick waves across his pillow. The night had been warm and humid, but she'd tucked the sheet around her lower half, conscious of her legs even after everything they'd done together—all the ways he'd explored her—over the last twenty hours.

He didn't understand her insecurity. Marietta was a beautiful, sensual woman and he didn't give a damn about her legs.

He curled a thick strand of dark lustrous hair around his fingers. He'd known his attraction to her was strong, but he hadn't predicted just how fiercely and completely his hunger for her would consume him. He had the feeling she had been seared into his memory for life—and yet he knew the danger of collecting memories. Knew how treacherous they could be. How they could lurk in your soul, lying in wait for the moment when you finally thought you were strong and then raising their insidious heads just so they could remind you of what you'd once had— what you'd lost.

Marietta's eyelids fluttered open and she turned her head, blinked sleepy, liquid brown eyes at him.

Nico shook off his maudlin thoughts, curved his mouth into a smile. 'Morning, *ma petite sirène.*'

She stretched her arms above her head. 'What does that mean?'

'My little mermaid.'

She blinked, took a moment to process that, then turned her face towards the window. An adorable scowl formed on her face. 'It can't be morning.'

'It is,' he assured her. 'Late morning, in fact.' He circled a fingertip around her left nipple and the nub of caramel flesh puckered and hardened. 'Time to wake up.'

She stretched again, shamelessly thrusting those perfect breasts towards him. 'Coffee...' she mumbled. 'Mermaids need coffee to wake up.'

He took her hand and guided it to his groin. 'I have something better than coffee to wake you up.'

Her eyes flared, her lips parted—and suddenly his little mermaid didn't look sleepy any more.

Over the next forty-eight hours time slowed and blurred and the outside world ceased to exist—or at least that was how it felt to Marietta. They made love at regular intervals and in between they ate and swam, either at the beach or in the pool. When Nico disappeared to his study every so often to work she would paint, parking herself in front of her canvas and the easel which he'd erected for her in a sunlit corner of the living room.

In no time at all she started feeling as though she were living in one of those protective bubbles, the thought of which she'd scoffed at only nights before. Which was dangerous, she knew. Bubbles were pretty, but they were temporary. Sooner or later they burst—and hers was about to burst very soon. Because it was Thursday afternoon, and that meant that tomorrow she would return to Rome.

A good thing too, she told herself, slotting tubes of paint into their storage container. This thing with Nico couldn't last. A few days of indulgence—that was all it was meant to be. He'd been up-front about that, and so had she.

She had a life to return to. An excellent, satisfying life where there was no room, no need, for unrealistic expectations.

Plus she had little Ricci's party in two days' time. That would cheer her up. Help her get rid of this silly ache which had settled in her chest this morning and so far had refused to budge.

Nico appeared in the doorway of the living room. He'd been working in his study for no more than an hour and still her breath hitched as if she were seeing him for the first time in days.

She smiled, forced herself to sound brighter than she felt. 'I thought I'd get a head start on packing up my things. I assume we'll leave early in the morning?'

'We're not,' he said.

She paused in the process of wrapping her brushes in a cloth. 'Oh…? What time *will* we leave, then?'

'We're not leaving.'

She blinked at him, and for a fraction of a second her heart soared. Because if they weren't leaving then she wouldn't have to say goodbye to him just yet. She wouldn't sleep with him tonight knowing it was the last time they would ever make love. The last time she would ever feel him inside her, filling her. Making her feel beautiful and desirable and wanton and *whole*.

And then her brain reasserted itself. 'What do you mean, we're not leaving?'

'Exactly that.' He came into the room. 'You're not going back to Rome tomorrow.'

His tone left no room for misinterpretation. He wasn't giving her a choice. He was *telling* her.

For the first time in days, her temper flared. She put her brushes down. 'One week, Nico. I agreed to come here for *one week*.'

He crossed his arms over his chest. The gesture reminded her of the way he and Leo had confronted her six days ago. How they had bulldozed her into coming here. She'd been angry, hating the loss of her independence, the sense of having control of her life stripped away. Which was why she'd laid down her own rules—rules Nico was now completely ignoring.

'Until your stalker is caught, this is the safest place for you to be.'

She folded her arms, mirroring his pose with an equally resolute one of her own. 'And *when* will you catch him?' she demanded to know. 'Next week? Next *month*?'

Something glittered in his eyes. 'Is that an appalling idea, *chérie*? Spending an entire month with me?'

She pressed her lips together before she could blurt out the word *no*. The idea didn't appal her. Not in the slightest. In fact it made her feel light-headed. Euphoric. And that was wrong.

Wrong, wrong, *wrong*.

She wasn't *meant* to want more of him.

'This is hardly a joking matter,' she said. 'I have a job to get back to. A *life*. And it's my nephew's first birthday party on Saturday—I told Leo and Helena I wouldn't miss it.'

'I've spoken with Leo and he agrees you should stay.'

Her anger bloomed, swift and bright and vivid like a bloodstain on cotton. *How dared they?* 'That's not Leo's decision to make—nor, might I add, is it yours!'

She seized the wheels of her chair and propelled herself towards the doorway.

'Where are you going?'

'To call my sister-in-law,' she snapped.

'Why?'

'Because she's got more sense than you and my brother put together!'

And maybe Helena could change her husband's

mind. If Marietta had Leo on her side Nico would have to let her go—a thought that only sharpened the ache in her chest.

And that made her angrier still.

Sisterhood, it turned out, was overrated.

Helena had sided with the men. Marietta had wanted to express her anger over the phone but found she couldn't. Her sister-in-law's stance came from a place of caring and concern, and Marietta wasn't angry with Helena. She was angry at the situation— and with Nico for his high-handedness. He hadn't even consulted her first. He'd simply made the decision.

She managed a smile for the young waitress who had arrived at the table with her dessert and then realised the courtesy was a wasted effort. The girl was more interested in casting pretty smiles at Nico, even though she looked as if she was barely out of her teens and he was surely too old for her.

He had that powerful effect on women. She imagined he always would. He'd carry those rugged good looks and that dark sex appeal into his later years and become one of those sexy, distinguished-looking older men to whom women of all ages flocked.

The thought didn't improve Marietta's mood.

And if Nico had hoped a nice meal and the buoyant atmosphere of the Bouchards' seaside restaurant would, he was in for disappointment. She picked up her spoon and cracked the hard caramelised top of her *crème brûlée* with a sharp jab.

'You're still angry.'

She glanced across the table at him. He was clean-shaven for the first time in two days and the skin over his hard jaw looked bronzed and taut in the golden candlelight which flickered from the glass holder on the table.

'Of course,' she said, opting for honesty, because no matter how hard she strove for the kind of composure she'd often admired in her sister-in-law she'd never been very good at hiding her emotions. 'I'm missing an important family event by staying here, Nico.'

His long fingers toyed with his espresso cup. 'You would put a child's birthday party above your own safety?'

'It's not just any child's party,' she retorted. 'It's my *nephew's* very first birthday and a milestone I won't get to share with him now.'

Nico regarded her. 'It means that much to you?'

'*Si.*'

She laid down the spoon. *Crème brûlée* was her favourite dessert, but she didn't really have the stomach for its rich creaminess right now. The only reason she'd ordered it was to delay the end of their meal and their return to the house. If their post-dinner entertainment followed the trend of the last two evenings they would very quickly end up naked—and she didn't want that to happen. Not yet. She wanted to nurse her anger awhile longer and she knew that as soon as he touched her, the second he was deep inside her, she'd forget she was supposed to be angry with him.

'They're my family,' she added, sitting back in her wheelchair. 'The only family I'll ever have.'

His eyes narrowed. 'What do you mean?'

She shrugged, but inwardly she cringed. That statement had been too honest. Too revealing. 'Exactly that,' she said, tossing his words from that afternoon back at him.

He looked at her for a long moment. 'Can you not have children, Marietta?' he asked quietly, and the intimacy of the question—from a man who routinely avoided conversations of a personal nature—threw her.

She hesitated. 'There's no medical reason I can't have children,' she admitted, pushing her dessert plate away. 'It's possible…physically.'

His gaze narrowed further. 'So there's nothing stopping you from having a family of your own?'

Her chest tightened. He made it sound so natural. So easy. As if having a broken back didn't make her different. 'It's not that simple,' she said, her voice stilted.

'Why?'

She frowned at him. Around them the restaurant was busy, with the clink of tableware, the buzz of conversation and frequent bouts of laughter lending the place a lively air. Josephine had seated them at a private table, however, set in a quiet corner by a large window overlooking the harbour.

Marietta glanced around, assuring herself that their conversation wasn't being overheard. 'Generally speaking, a woman needs a husband before she has children,' she said.

He lifted an eyebrow. 'And you object to marriage?'

Her frown deepened. Why was he asking her these questions? Why was he interested?

Why should he *care?*

Her breath caught in her throat.

Did he care?

Hastily she crushed the thought. He was making conversation, showing a polite interest in the woman he was temporarily sleeping with.

She cleared her throat. 'Marriage is fine,' she said. 'It's just not for me.'

'Because of Davide?'

'Partly.' She lifted her shoulder. 'When push comes to shove, few men want to tie themselves to a cripple for life.'

Nico's brows slammed down, his face darkening. 'Don't call yourself that,' he said tersely.

'What? A cripple?' She affected an air of indifference. 'Why not? That's how most people see me.'

Which wasn't strictly true. She was fortunate; she

had people in her life who saw the woman first and foremost and not the disability. But equally there were those who *never* saw beyond the wheelchair. Never saw *her*.

Blue eyes blazed at her from across the table. 'That's not how *I* see you.'

Her heart lurched. She believed him, but how *did* he see her? As a woman who needed protecting? A perk of the job? She'd already guessed she was one of a long string of short-term lovers he'd taken in the years since his wife's death. She'd told herself it didn't matter to her, ignored the taunting voice that had cried *liar*.

'I know,' she said quietly.

Nico's gaze stayed pinned on her. 'Davide was an idiot,' he said. 'But he's one man. Why write off your dreams because of one bad experience?'

Her shoulders stiffened. 'Because I'm a realist—and some things simply aren't destined to be.' She sniffed. 'Anyway, you have no idea *what* my dreams are. Not every woman longs for the white picket fence, you know.'

He raised his eyebrows. 'So you don't *want* children?'

'No.' But that was a lie. A lie she had repeated in her head so often she'd almost believed it. Her stomach knotted.

'But family is important to you?'

'So are other things,' she said, hating the defensive note in her voice. 'My job—my career as an artist...'

She trailed off. Her words had sounded hollow and they shouldn't have. She was utterly passionate about her art. Determined to make a full-time living from it eventually. In the meantime she had a job she loved, her apartment, her studio for hire... It was enough. Of *course* it was enough.

So why had Nico's questions got her all tied up in knots?

She took the white napkin off her lap, folded it carefully and placed it on the table. 'Thank you for dinner,' she said, avoiding his eye. 'I'm ready to go when you are.'

The Bouchards came out to farewell them, dropping kisses onto Marietta's cheeks, and she wondered what assumptions they'd made about her and Nico's relationship.

Not that it mattered. Sooner or later she'd be gone from Île de Lavande and she'd have no reason to return—a thought she found inordinately depressing as Nico drove them home on the winding mountain road. When they arrived, he parked in the courtyard by the house, went to open the front door, then returned and lifted her out of the Jeep. He carried her towards the house.

'Nico!' she cried. 'My chair!'

He kicked the front door closed, barely breaking stride. 'You won't be needing it for a while.'

Outrage and something else she didn't want to acknowledge sent a lick of heat through her veins.

Her voice rose on a high note of fury. 'I'm *not* sleeping with you tonight!'

He reached his bedroom and dropped her unceremoniously onto his bed, so that she sprawled inelegantly on the grey silk coverlet.

He shot her a dark, blistering look and started unbuttoning his shirt. 'I don't plan on doing much sleeping.'

She pushed onto her elbows, glared up at him. 'I'm still angry with you!' she flung at him.

He shrugged off his shirt and threw it to the floor. The moonlight illuminating the room washed over his powerful torso, making him look like a statue of some demigod cast in pewter.

Marietta's mouth dried.

'Bien,' he said in a low, rough voice, simultaneously toeing off his shoes and unbuckling his belt. 'I like that fiery temper.'

He shoved the rest of his clothes off and when he straightened the full extent of his arousal was plain to see. He curled his hand around himself and the sight of him doing so was deeply erotic. Utterly mesmerising.

'It turns me on,' he said, quite unnecessarily, and then he was climbing onto the bed.

She shook herself, shot her arm out and slapped her palm against his chest. 'Stop!'

'You don't mean that,' he said, and his lips curved into a smile of such utter carnality that her belly flooded with hot, liquid need. Then he pushed up her top, freed her left breast from its lacy confines and sucked her nipple into his mouth.

Marietta gasped, her traitorous body arching in response to the exquisite sensations he inflicted so effortlessly. She lifted her hands, intending to beat them down upon his bare shoulders, but somehow her fingers ended up buried in his thick hair.

His head lifted, his blue eyes glittering with triumph. 'Do you still want me to stop?'

She gave him a mutinous glare, then dragged his head down and kissed him, sinking her teeth into his lower lip for a second before pushing his head back up.

'This won't make me forget that I'm angry with you,' she warned him.

That wicked smile returned, making her insides quiver.

'Chérie,' he said, lowering himself on top of her, his hard body crushing her into the mattress, 'by the time I'm done with you, you won't remember your *name.*'

CHAPTER TEN

'DID I DRAG you out of bed, my friend?'

Leo Vincenti's voice carried over the video feed with a distinct note of dryness.

Nico thrust his hand through his dishevelled hair and peered at his friend's image on his computer screen. Leo sat in his office in Rome, looking immaculate in a crisp shirt and tie, making Nico even more aware of his unshaved jaw and the rumpled tee shirt he'd hurriedly pulled on after realising he was late for the video call he and Leo had scheduled for this morning.

'Long night working,' he said as he ruthlessly smothered the image of his friend's sister naked and spread-eagled on his bed.

Dieu. He hadn't considered how truly awkward it would be to look his friend in the eye after all the things he had done with Marietta last night.

Never had he known sex to be so... so *combustible.* So all-consuming. And still he wanted more. Still his groin twitched at the mere thought of sliding between her thighs and burying himself inside her wet, welcoming heat.

He moved his chair closer to the desk, concealing his lower body.

'Sorry I couldn't talk longer yesterday,' said Leo. 'I was in the middle of a client crisis meeting. You said you had more news?'

'There's been a development,' Nico confirmed, forcing his mind away from the sleepy, satisfied woman he'd left in his bed. He'd placed her chair within arm's reach, in case she wanted to get up, but he hoped she'd stay put. He wasn't finished with her yet.

He sat forward and gave a brief summary of the information Bruno had imparted yesterday. Late on Wednesday one of the two men they'd shortlisted as suspects had confronted Lina at the gallery and demanded to know Marietta's whereabouts. When Lina had claimed not to know he'd become aggressive and physical. Bruno was convinced they had their man. But now the guy had gone to ground.

Leo's expression was grim. 'Is the girl all right?'

'She's fine. I have a protective detail on her.'

'How will you find him?'

'We have the *polizia* fully on board now.' And his own men continued to work around the clock.

'Does Marietta know?'

'Not yet.' When the perpetrator was in custody—*then* he would tell her. In the meantime she didn't need to know about Lina. She'd only worry. 'I'll give her the details when the time is right.'

Leo dragged a hand over his face, pulled in a deep breath. 'Thank you, Nico,' he said gravely. 'I don't know how I can ever repay you for this.'

Nico shrugged. 'If our roles were reversed you would do the same, *mon ami*,' he said, tamping down on a flare of guilt.

Marietta was a grown woman, he reminded himself. She wasn't answerable to her brother—and neither was he.

He promised Leo to keep him updated and disconnected the call. When he returned to the bedroom Marietta was still in bed, early-morning sunlight streaming over her mahogany hair and golden breasts. He shed his clothes and climbed in beside her.

She stirred, blinked those beautiful dark eyes at him. 'I thought I heard you talking to someone...'

'Just a work call,' he said, cupping a soft, lush breast in his hand and thumbing its nipple. She moaned, and the little nub of caramel flesh peaked into a hard point that begged for the attention of his mouth.

A few more days, he acknowledged, his heart punching hard at the thought. That was all he'd have with her. Right then it didn't seem as if it could possibly be enough, but it would have to be. He had nothing to give her beyond these days on the island, nothing to offer, and she deserved more. She deserved a man capable of love. A man who would tear down the barriers she didn't even know she'd erected around herself and convince her she'd make an amazing wife and mother.

Nico wasn't that man. And for a moment, as he stared into her liquid brown eyes, the knowledge twisted his stomach into a knot of deep, gut-wrenching regret.

Marietta lay on her side on the soft beach rug and watched the steady rise and fall of Nico's magnificent chest as he slept.

He wore only a pair of swimming trunks and she trailed her gaze over his bronzed body, her belly twisting with a physical need she'd thought might have lessened over the last three days but had, in fact, only intensified.

They'd settled into something of a routine. In the mornings they'd linger in bed and make love, before indulging in a leisurely breakfast on the terrace, then Nico would work for two to three hours in his study and Marietta would paint. When her tummy grumbled she'd wash out her brushes and make them some lunch, and afterwards they'd swim and laze by the pool or at the beach. Dinner was usually a light snack, shared at the kitchen table or out on the terrace—and bedtime always came early.

It was indulgent and idyllic and it couldn't last.

Marietta knew that, and that was why she planned to enjoy it. Reality would intrude soon enough. For now she was going to accept these extra days with Nico for what she'd decided they were—once her anger over missing Ricci's birthday had worn off. A gift.

She traced her finger over the words tattooed around the emblem on his left arm. *Honneur et Fidélité*. It was the motto of the French Foreign Legion and somehow those words—honour and fidelity— fitted him perfectly. Because he *was* loyal and honourable. Her brother had said so many times, and Leo trusted him implicitly—as did she.

Her heart squeezed every time she thought about what he'd revealed of his childhood. She ached inside for the lonely boy he must have been, and she ached for the man he was now—a man who held himself aloof from the world. A man who seemed very much alone.

He was like a multi-layered gift-wrapped parcel, she decided. The kind that was passed around a circle of children at a party and when the music stopped another layer was unceremoniously ripped off. The excitement—and the frustration—was in not knowing how many layers there would be. Not knowing exactly when you were going to peel off the final layer and reach the heart of the parcel—the true gift beneath.

Nico had many layers—most of them deeply buried. His difficult childhood, the loss of his mother, his time as a soldier and the horrors he must have seen... But she sensed his greatest trauma—and thus the key to understanding him—had been the loss of his wife, and unfortunately that subject had been declared off-limits.

'Ready for a swim, *ma petite sirène?*'

She jumped, her hand jerking away from his arm.

Of course he hadn't been asleep.

She smiled at the endearment. *My little mermaid.* When she swam with him she *felt* like a mermaid, too. Graceful and elegant. Playful and sultry. For a while she'd forget all about her useless legs and simply revel in the freedom of the water. The exquisite pleasure of being skin to skin with him.

'In a bit,' she said, tracing her finger through the dark, crisp hair on his forearm.

Her mind toyed with the question.

Did she dare?

She looked at him, then took a deep breath and plunged in. 'Will you tell me about your wife?'

He tensed, and she held her breath.

He sat up, the lines of his shoulders and back rigid.

'I asked you never to speak about that.'

'I know, but—'

'Leave it, Marietta.'

She swallowed. 'I only—'

'I said *leave it.*'

And he lunged to his feet, stalked across the sand and dived into the water.

* * *

When Nico emerged from the sea he had no idea
how long he'd been swimming. Fifteen minutes, if he
hazarded a guess. Twenty at the most. Long enough
for regret to outweigh his anger.

He had been too harsh with Marietta. These last
few days they had been totally absorbed in one another, as physically intimate as two people could be.
Her curiosity had felt intrusive, uncomfortable—
more than uncomfortable—but it wasn't entirely un-
reasonable.

He padded across the sand. She lay on her back
now, the awning shading her from the afternoon sun,
her enormous dark sunglasses keeping her eyes hidden. A bright blue sarong draped her legs and she
wore the yellow bikini top he'd enjoyed removing
on numerous occasions. She must have heard his approach and yet she didn't move a muscle.

He dropped to his knees on the rug and shook his
head, spraying droplets of seawater over her.

'Hey!' She whipped her sunglasses off and glared
up at him.

He stared back, meeting that fiery little temper of
hers head-on. 'You're upset,' he observed.

'You got up and walked away from me, Nico.
How do you *think* that makes me feel? Knowing that
I can't stand up and follow you?'

Shame pierced him, and he didn't like it. 'You
pushed me, Marietta,' he said, taking a defensive tack.

'I asked you a question. That's all.'

Frustration needled under his skin. He grabbed a towel, dried himself off and sat down beside her. He stared moodily out at the sea. 'I don't talk about my wife with other people.'

A pause. 'Is that what I am to you?' she asked quietly. '"Other people"?'

He turned his head to look at her. 'No,' he conceded gruffly—because she wasn't. She was different—the only person he'd let get this close to him in ten years.

Hell. He pushed his hands through his hair, closed his eyes for a moment. Then he stretched out on his back beside her and took a deep, slow breath.

'Her name was Julia,' he began, 'and we met at a resort in Mexico when I was twenty-four.'

He could feel Marietta's gaze on him but he kept his own pinned on the blue and white stripes of the awning above them.

'She was vacationing with girlfriends and I was blowing off steam with some guys I had just completed a private security contract with.'

It had been a classic case of 'opposites attract'. He'd been a big, rough-around-the-edges foreigner and she'd been a pretty polished blonde from a privileged background. But Julia had been so much more than that. She had been sweetness and light—everything Nico had missed from his life since his mother had died.

Within six months they'd been married, despite her parents' protestations.

'It should never have worked,' he said. 'Our backgrounds were too different. And her father was running for the state senate.' He grimaced at the memory of Jack Lewisham's reaction to the man his daughter had declared she was marrying. 'I wasn't exactly desirable son-in-law material.'

He paused. Marietta was silent, but he sensed her listening intently.

'Things were rocky with her parents at the start, but eventually they accepted me.'

Nico had been determined to prove to Jack Lewisham that he was worthy of the man's daughter. He'd worked multiple day jobs and studied for a business degree at night, with the intention of starting his own company. In the end Jack had been impressed. He'd even loaned Nico a substantial chunk of capital to get the business started.

He closed his eyes and swallowed, his mouth going dry.

'Julia was kidnapped.'

Marietta gasped. *'Mio Dio...'* she breathed. 'By whom?'

'Opportunists. Criminals.' His jaw hardened. 'Her parents were extremely wealthy and high-profile.'

'Oh, Nico...'

He could hear the horror in her voice, blocked it out.

'Her father and I argued over whether or not to involve the authorities. The kidnappers had warned against it and Jack was terrified. He believed that his willingness to hand over the ransom combined with my military experience and resources would be sufficient to get Julia home safely.' He clenched his jaw. 'The man practically got on his knees and begged me to agree.'

'And you did?'

'Reluctantly.'

The absolute worst decision of his life. His biggest, most horrific failure.

She touched his arm. 'What happened?'

'Julia was shot.'

Marietta's hand tightened on his arm, communicating her shock, and somehow her touch grounded him. Kept him from sliding back to that dark place in his head where there was only that filthy ditch and Julia's cold, lifeless body.

'Were the kidnappers caught?' she asked gently.

'Eventually.'

He hadn't rested—not until every member of the gang responsible had been caught, prosecuted and imprisoned.

'They claimed her death had been an accident. Said she'd made a grab for one of their guns and it went off in a struggle.'

'Nico… I'm so sorry…'

Finally he looked at her. Tears streaked her face and he muttered a curse, gathered her into his arms.

'Please tell me you don't blame yourself,' she whispered, pressing her face to his chest.

In the silence that followed she lifted her head and stared at him.

'Nico! You can't possibly—'

'I can,' he said grimly. 'And so did Jack.'

'But that's crazy—how *could* he?'

'He was a man half-demented with grief.' It was something Nico had understood, for he, too, had almost lost his mind. 'He needed to lash out. To blame someone other than himself.'

Marietta put her head back on his chest. 'It wasn't your fault,' she said fiercely.

Nico tightened his arms around her. She was, he thought with an odd feeling of gratitude, the only person ever to try to absolve him of guilt.

For the first time in days Nico retired to his study after dinner, and when it got late and he still hadn't emerged Marietta went to bed alone.

She lay in his gigantic bed, thinking of everything he'd told her on the beach that day, and her heart ached for him.

How could he blame himself for his wife's death? And how could his father-in-law blame him for a decision the older man had essentially made himself?

It didn't make sense—but when did these kinds

of things ever make sense? It was the nature of trag-
edies. Of how people tried to cope. And she understood something about that. Her friends had died
in the accident and she hadn't—how could she not
have questioned that outcome? Not felt some degree
of survivor's guilt? But in the end she'd had to let it
go or it would have destroyed her. She had decided
to be strong. To make something of her life—of the
second chance her young friends had been so cruelly denied.

And are you? a voice in her head challenged. *Are
you making the most of that chance?*

She frowned at the ceiling. She had tried hard for
the last three days not to think about her conversation with Nico at the restaurant. He'd pushed some
buttons she'd thought were no longer sensitive. Re-
kindled a longing for things she had convinced herself were out of reach.

But she knew that yearning for things that might
never be was dangerous. A guarantee of heartache
and disappointment. She had already travelled that
road—with the experimental surgeries, with Davide... She couldn't set herself on a path of false
hope again.

Which made the little daydreams she'd caught
herself indulging in these past few days—silly fantasised scenarios of wheeling down a church aisle in
a white gown, or holding a tiny sweet-smelling baby
in her arms—all the more ridiculous.

The sound of footsteps coming down the hallway halted her thoughts. Quickly she closed her eyes, feigned sleep. If Nico had wanted to make love to her tonight he'd have joined her sooner; she had too much pride to let him think she'd been lying here waiting for him.

She heard the rustle of clothes being shed, felt the bed compress and then, to her surprise, the press of a hot palm against her breast. She looked up and saw the glitter of blue eyes in the semi-darkness before his mouth claimed hers in a hard, invasive kiss that drove a hot spike of need through her core.

He pushed her thighs apart, slid his hand between her legs and growled low in his throat when he found her wet and ready for him. He rolled away for a moment and then he was back, braced above her this time, his features stark, the glitter in his eyes ferocious as he entered her with a single powerful thrust.

She gasped his name, clinging to his shoulders as he drove deep, again and again. He had never taken her hard and fast like this before—as though he barely had control of himself—and she thrilled to the wild, primitive feeling of being claimed.

Possessed.

She dug her fingers into rippling muscle, feeling the tension and the heat building, spiralling, until a moan rushed up her throat and she crested that blinding peak at the same instant as Nico's big body tensed above her. He slammed deep into her one last time and pleasure pulsated from her core, obliterating every conscious thought from her head except for one.

One thought that stopped her heart as his weight bore down on her and she wrapped her arms tightly around him.

She loved him.

Marietta put down her brush and studied the canvas. The painting was finally finished and she was pleased with it. Her choice of colours and the way she'd illustrated the fortress's proud, crumbling ruins, with pale shafts of sunlight slanting through the old ramparts, had created the impression of something ethereal, almost otherworldly.

But she couldn't help but wish now that she'd painted something different. Something a little brighter, more uplifting. She had planned on leaving the painting behind—as a gift for Nico—but it seemed too haunting now for a man who was already haunted.

A shiver rippled through her. Their lovemaking last night had been so intense. So *silent*. Nico hadn't uttered a word—not before or during or afterwards—and yet he'd watched her the entire time he had been inside her, with that fierce intensity blazing in his blue eyes.

Her heart twisted painfully in her chest. The emotion she'd been wrestling with ever since her shattering revelation last night refused to be subdued.

She could *not* have fallen in love with him. Not so quickly. So hopelessly. So irrevocably.

Except she had.

And now her heart would break, because she wanted something she couldn't have. *A man.* A man too closed off from his emotions to ever be available to her or anyone else.

And already he was withdrawing.

He hadn't reached for her this morning…hadn't lavished her with kisses and caresses while the sun rose and then joined her for a lazy breakfast on the terrace. Instead he'd got dressed and gone straight to his study, emerging only for a quick lunch before disappearing again.

She put her paints away and folded her brushes into a rag for cleaning. The ache in her chest was her penance, she told herself harshly. She'd been a fool and now she'd have to live with the consequences— a concept she was all too familiar with.

She wheeled down the hall towards the utility room where she usually cleaned her brushes.

Nico stepped out of his study.

'Do you have a minute?'

She stopped and looked at him. He sounded so *polite*. The ache in her chest intensified. For the last three days she'd deliberately avoided asking about her stalker, assuring herself that Nico would tell her anything important.

He had something important to tell her now. Which meant this was the beginning of the end.

Her mouth drying, she nodded, and he stood back so she could wheel herself into the study. She stopped by his desk and he handed her a piece of paper—a printed digital photograph of a man.

'Do you know him?'

She studied the image. The man was clean-shaven, and he wore trendy thin-rimmed eyeglasses and a baseball cap. The photograph was grainy, as if it had been enlarged a few times, but the man's face was clear enough and...*familiar*.

She nodded slowly. 'It's Sergio Berardi. He's an artist.' She studied the photo again, an icy finger sliding across her nape. 'I exhibited some of his work at the gallery about a year ago.'

'Nine months,' said Nico.

The hairs on her arms lifted. 'I've met him a few times socially, through art circles,' she said, and suddenly it all made a horrible kind of sense. She put the photo down on the desk, not wanting to look at it any longer. 'He asked me out a couple of times but I declined.'

He hadn't been unpleasant, or unattractive, but she'd already decided not to waste her time on relationships. She rubbed her forehead. Thinking back, he *had* been intense. A little unsettling.

'*Santo cielo…*' Bile climbed her throat. 'I can't believe I didn't think of him before.'

Nico shrugged, as if it were of no consequence. 'Don't beat yourself up,' he said.

Did he sound distant, or was she imagining it? Being oversensitive?

Her heart lurched. She wanted to rewind. Go back to the beginning and relive her time with him. Relive the fantasy. Because she knew with utter certainty that her life wouldn't be the same when she got back to Rome. Not after Nico.

She swallowed past the lump in her throat. 'What happens now?'

'I'm leaving immediately for Toulon.'

She frowned up at him. 'Don't you mean *we* are leaving?'

'*Non,*' he said. 'I need to get to Rome as quickly as possible, to liaise with the authorities. I can travel faster if I leave at once and go on my own. I'll do a quick round trip and be back late tomorrow. We can stay here tomorrow night and then get you back to Rome on Wednesday.'

One last night with him.

Her heart somersaulted. 'Okay,' she agreed—too readily.

He glanced at his watch. '*Bien.* I'll call Josephine. See if she or Luc are available to come and collect you.' He started gathering together papers on his desk. 'You should go and pack an overnight bag straight away.'

Marietta blinked at him. 'Why would I do that?'

He paused. 'Because you'll be staying at Josephine's tonight.'

She blinked again. 'And why would I do that when I can stay here?'

He frowned. 'Because I don't want you staying here on your own.'

She stared at him. 'Why not? I live alone in Rome. You *know* that, Nico. I'm more than capable of spending a night here on my own.'

'Rome is different. You live in an urban apartment, with neighbours and people nearby. It's too isolated up here. I want to know you're safe while I'm gone.'

'You mean you want someone to babysit me?' Her face heated with indignation. 'I'm paralysed, Nico—not *useless*.'

His expression darkened. 'I did not say you were useless.'

'But you might as well have. Heaven forbid the poor cripple is left to fend for herself!'

Now his face turned thunderous. 'Don't call yourself a cripple!'

'Then don't *treat* me like one!'

'Marietta…' His voice was a low, warning growl.

She pushed her chin up. 'I'm staying here.'

He cursed loudly. 'I don't have time for this.'

'No, you don't,' she agreed. 'So I suggest you get a move on and go and pack *your* bag.'

A nerve flickered in his temple. He opened his mouth and closed it again, then scowled and stalked out of the room.

Nico sat in a leather recliner in his private jet and stared out at the thickening wall of cloud as the aircraft's powerful engines ate up the miles to Toulon.

It was twenty-six hours since he'd left for Rome and he was eager to get back to Île dc Lavande. Leaving Marietta alone at the house had not sat well with him, but she was proud—stubborn as hell—and she'd argued him into a corner.

He stretched out his legs, rubbed eyes that felt gritty and strained. Dealing with endless police bureaucracy in Rome and the vagaries of the Italian legal system had been an exercise in frustration. But he'd called on some old contacts, pulled a few strings and in the end got what he'd wanted: a little one-on-one time in a non-surveillance holding cell with Sergio Berardi.

Nico hadn't laid a finger on the man and he hadn't needed to. Berardi had nearly wet himself the second Nico had locked the door, shrugged off his jacket and rolled up his sleeves. He intended to do everything within his power to ensure that the charges against Berardi stuck and he was locked up, but Nico had wanted to make certain that in the event the man was released he understood *exactly* what kind of retribution to expect if he went anywhere near Marietta.

He swallowed a mouthful of whisky.

He had missed Marietta last night. Missed her sweet, intoxicating smell, her soft warmth, the taste of her lingering on his tongue after making love. Even thinking about her now sent a powerful throb of desire pulsing through him.

Mon Dieu.

He'd crossed a line with her but he couldn't bring himself to regret it. Marietta had been a balm to his tortured soul. A ray of light in the sea of darkness that had closed over his head a long time ago.

He took another gulp of whisky.

Perhaps he was being hasty, confining their affair to these few days on the island? He couldn't imagine his hunger for her dying any time soon—nor could he imagine another woman satisfying him while his need for Marietta still burned in his blood. He could see her occasionally, could he not? A casual arrangement might be the perfect solution. Might suit them both until—

A massive jolt wrenched Nico sideways in his seat. His head hit the wall and the glass flew from his hand, whisky spilling everywhere and soaking the crotch of his trousers. He swore, looked up, and saw his flight attendant, Evelyn, clutching a seatback. He barked at her to sit down and strap herself in, then picked up the built-in handset that gave him direct access to the cockpit.

'Severe unexpected turbulence, sir,' his pilot informed him. 'It's the edge of a category three storm—coming through a couple of hours earlier than expected.'

Expected? Nico swore again. He always checked the weather forecasts when he was headed to the island. *Always.* But this time… This time he'd forgotten. He'd been preoccupied. Distracted.

'We have clearance from Toulon, provided we land in the next fifteen minutes,' the pilot advised. 'After that everything's grounded or diverted.'

Which meant he had zero chance of flying the chopper to the island. He stared grimly out of the window. The cloud was menacing and black, darkening the interior of the plane.

'What direction is the storm coming from?'

The pilot rattled off the latest update—and Nico felt the blood drain from his face.

The storm was headed straight for Île de Lavande.

CHAPTER ELEVEN

THE PHONE LINE was dead.

With clammy hands Marietta put the receiver back in its cradle on Nico's desk.

This is just some bad weather, she told herself for the umpteenth time—then jumped as the entire house shifted and groaned under the onslaught of the powerful wind. She looked out of the window at the angry sky. *Dark.* It was so dark. Yet it was only late afternoon. She tried the light switch in the study, then a couple out in the hall—nothing. The house had no power.

Dio. Please let Nico be safe, she prayed. He wouldn't do anything crazy, would he? Like try to fly in this weather?

She wheeled herself to a window in the living room, looked out at the sea, which had been whipped into a seething grey-green frenzy, then back at the clouds—which looked wilder, even blacker now if that were possible.

No. Of course Nico wouldn't try to fly in this. He was too safety-conscious. Too sensible.

If only *she* had been sensible. If only she hadn't argued with him. If only she hadn't been so stubborn and proud and oversensitive about her independence. She could have been warm and comfortable with the Bouchards right now. Instead she was here. Alone and, yes—she'd swallow her pride and admit it—*just a tiny bit terrified.*

Rain came down—thick, horizontal sheets of it lashing the glass—and the wind roared like some kind of vicious animal howling for blood. It raised the hairs on Marietta's nape. Made her want to curl up in Nico's bed, pull the covers over her head and breathe in his scent. Pretend that he was there and she was wrapped in his strong arms, protected and safe.

She pulled in a deep breath.

Nico wouldn't travel in this storm. She was alone—at least for tonight. Which meant she'd need to be calm, practical. Prepared. She'd start by looking for a torch, she decided. Then she'd recheck the windows and doors to make sure the house was secure, and hunt out some candles and matches.

She found a lantern torch in the utility room and started her check of the house in the study. She wheeled to the window and glanced out—just as the large terrace table at which she and Nico had shared so many meals by the pool started to slide across the limestone pavers. Her eyes rounded with disbelief. The table was heavy—a solid piece of outdoor furniture—yet it might as well have been plastic for all its resistance to the wind.

Her heart surged into her throat as another wild gust shook the walls—and then the table simply lifted into the air like a piece of driftwood and flew towards the house.

Marietta backed her chair away as fast as she could and spun around. But the torch slipped off her lap and caught under her wheel. Her chair lurched and tipped and she threw her arms out to break her fall, crashing to the floor at the same moment as the table slammed into the study window. She locked her arms over her head, protecting her face from the splintered glass that showered all around her.

Fear clawed at her chest and a sob punched out of her throat. Clapping her hands over her ears, she tried to block out the violent cacophony of wind and rain. And started to pray.

Nico paced the floor of his hotel room in Toulon.

The room was tiny, compared to the hotel suites he normally stayed in, but the city was full of stranded travellers and last-minute accommodation was scarce. Not that he cared one iota about the room. He barely noticed the tired decor and frayed furnishings. Barely registered the cramped confines that forced him to spin on his heel every ten steps and pace in the other direction.

The floor beneath him shook and the glass in the windows shuddered. The wind was gaining strength, becoming brutal in its capacity for damage even with the full force of the storm yet to hit the mainland. Toulon and the other coastal cities and towns were in a state of lockdown; in this part of Europe storms of this category were rare and people were cautious and nervous.

A cold sweat drenched his skin.

He was nervous.

He stopped. No. *Nervous* didn't do justice to what he was feeling right now.

He picked up his phone from the floor, where he'd thrown it earlier in a fit of fury and frustration. But he still couldn't get a connection; the network was either down or overloaded.

He tossed the phone aside.

His house was strong, he reminded himself. Architecturally designed and built to withstand the elements. And yet bricks and mortar were no match for Mother Nature at her worst. If she was so inclined she would demolish everything in her path.

Hell.

He resumed his pacing. *Josephine.* Josephine and her family knew Marietta was alone at the house. He'd called his housekeeper yesterday, before he'd left, to let her know—just as a precaution. The

Bouchards would check on Marietta, wouldn't they? If they'd been forewarned of the storm…

But the weather predictions had been wildly off— the storm was hitting land two hours sooner than expected…

Nico's head threatened to explode. He felt useless. Helpless. And he knew this feeling. He *knew* it. Remembered it. Had sworn he would never feel it again.

Suddenly Julia's face swam in his mind—laughing, eyes dancing…and then glassy, lifeless, her pale skin streaked with dirt. And cold. *So, so cold.*

His legs buckled beneath him and his knees slammed into the cheap carpet, the impact jarring his entire body.

Loving Julia had made him weak, left him open and defenceless, so that when the worst had happened—when she'd been taken from him—he'd had nothing inside him to fight the pain. And the pain, the agony of losing someone he'd loved, had nearly destroyed him.

Mon Dieu.

He couldn't do this again.

His mother.

Julia.

Marietta.

A wild, rage-filled roar tore from his throat and he picked up an ugly vase from the coffee table and hurled it across the room.

* * *

Marietta navigated her chair around the tree branches and clumps of debris strewn across the Bouchards' front yard and cast yet another anxious look towards the hills.

She couldn't see Nico's house from the village, but every so often throughout the morning she'd taken a break from helping in the kitchen to come outside and scour the skyline for signs of his chopper. Thankfully power had been restored to most of the village, but the phone lines were still down and mobile coverage was intermittent.

A gentle hand squeezed her shoulder. She looked up, and Josephine smiled down at her.

'He'll be fine.'

Marietta nodded. 'I know.'

Josephine gave her an understanding look. 'It is too easy to worry about the ones we love, *oui?*'

Marietta felt her smile stiffen. Was it really so obvious that she loved him?

'How are you feeling?' asked Josephine.

'Fine, thanks.'

And she *was* fine. She had a cut on her forehead, scratches on her arms and some bruises from falling out of her chair. But otherwise she was healthy and safe—thanks to Luc and Philippe, who had driven into the hills as the storm had descended on the island and rescued her.

She cast another look at the sky—a clear vivid

blue in the wake of the storm—and then returned with Josephine to the kitchen. They'd been baking all morning, preparing a mountain of food to sustain the men who were tackling the massive job of cleaning up the village.

It was good to feel useful, to do something constructive, but her thoughts kept drifting back to Nico.

She wanted more time with him. Wanted to explore the possibility of seeing him once she was back in Rome. It was crazy, and extending their affair would only delay the inevitable heartbreak, but she wanted it all the same. Because as much as her feelings for him frightened her, the thought of tonight being their very last together frightened her even more.

A commotion outside the house pulled Marietta from her thoughts. She paused with a tray of pastries in her hand and heard car doors slamming, then male voices speaking in rapid French. She thought she recognised Philippe's voice, deep and firm, and then another, even deeper but louder—and agitated.

Marietta almost dropped the tray.

Nico's voice.

Josephine had hurried outside and now Nico appeared in the doorway. And he looked—*terrible.* Bleary-eyed and unshaven, his hair and clothes rumpled. A hint of wildness in the blue eyes that instantly zeroed in on her. He reached her in three strides.

She put the tray down. 'I'm fine,' she said, hurriedly, because she could see that he wasn't and it was scaring her.

He didn't speak. He just tipped up her chin and examined the cut on her forehead, then lifted her arms, one by one, scrutinising the many nicks and scratches she'd sustained when the window had shattered over her. His mouth thinned.

'Nico, I'm *fine*,' she repeated, wanting to erase the awful bleakness from his face.

Still he didn't speak and his silence unnerved her.

'I'm afraid there's been some damage at the house,' she said. 'Your study—'

'I don't give a damn about the study.' Finally he spoke but his voice was harsh. Angry, even. 'I've already seen the house. I thought—' He broke off. '*Mon Dieu*, Marietta,' he resumed after a moment. 'I thought...' He dragged his hand through his hair, stepped back, his expression shuttering. 'Do you have any belongings to collect before we leave?'

'Just my clothes,' she said, referring to those she'd arrived in last night.

There'd been no time to grab anything else. When the men had found her in the study, Luc had scooped her off the floor while Philippe had grabbed her chair, and then they'd driven at once to the village. The clothes she wore now had been borrowed from Josephine who, minutes later, hovered as Nico bundled Marietta into the Jeep, followed by her chair and a bunch of supplies from Philippe for the house.

Marietta thanked the other woman—for every-thing—then sat in silence as Nico drove them back up the mountain.

Several hours later Nico's gut still churned with a mix of emotions, some clear-cut—like relief and anger—others not so easy to distinguish.

It had taken him two hours to clear the debris from the pool and terrace, another two to get the study back into some semblance of order. The re-pairs he'd made to the house were only temporary; he'd need a glazier to install a new window, some furnishings replaced and the flooring fixed, thanks to a fair amount of water damage.

The antique desk that had belonged to his wife had survived mostly unscathed, but in truth he had barely spared it a thought when he'd arrived at the house this morning and discovered the carnage. And—worse—Marietta gone. The violent punch of fear and panic had almost doubled him over. Until rational thought had resurfaced and he'd realised the only logical explanation was that she was in the vil-lage with the Bouchards.

He'd felt raw, volatile with emotion. So much so that he'd struggled for words when he'd first clapped eyes on her in the Bouchards' kitchen. On the drive back to the house, when she'd asked him what had happened in Rome, he'd managed to clip out a brief, sanitised version of events, but then he had kept his jaw tightly locked, afraid of what would spill from his mouth if he opened it again.

Since then he'd largely avoided her, rejecting her offer to help with the clean-up and suggesting she pack her things in preparation for leaving tomorrow. The hurt in her eyes had cut him to the bone, but it was safer this way. If he got too close to her he'd drag her into his arms and never want to let her go. And that terrified him.

Now, showered, wearing jeans and a fresh shirt, he stood in the living room and studied Marietta's painting of the old stone fortress. It was a stunning piece of work. Beautiful and evocative, he surmised. Not unlike the artist herself.

'Nico?'

He stiffened… *God help him.* Even the sound of her voice challenged his resolve. Made him think twice about what he must do.

'Nico, please…'

Her tone was plaintive and it tore at something inside him.

'Talk to me.'

He turned, hands jammed into his jeans pockets. 'What would you like me to say, Marietta?'

Long shafts of late-afternoon sunshine streamed in through the tall windows, gilding her olive skin, picking out the amber highlights in her mahogany hair. She'd changed out of the borrowed clothes into long black pants and a sleeveless white blouse and she looked beautiful. She *always* looked beautiful. She rolled closer and he clenched his jaw, fisted his hands to stop himself from reaching for her.

'You could start by telling me why you're angry.'

He shot her an incredulous look. Did she really have no idea what she'd put him through?

'I went through *hell* last night,' he bit out, his resolve to remain calm, impassive, flying out of the window. 'Knowing the storm was approaching and you were here alone while I was stuck on the mainland—' He broke off, jerked a hand out of his pocket and thrust it into his hair. '*Mon Dieu*, Marietta!'

She pulled her lower lip between her teeth. 'I can imagine how worried you must have been,' she said, and for some reason her placatory tone of voice only riled him further. 'I was worried about *you*, too,' she added. 'But we're both fine—aren't we?'

He begged to differ. He did *not* feel fine. He felt as if someone had mashed up his insides with a chain-saw. 'You could have been seriously injured—you *were* injured,' he ground out.

'A few scratches,' she dismissed. 'Nothing more.'

'Thanks to Luc and Philippe rescuing you—which they wouldn't have needed to do if you hadn't been so damned stubborn and insisted on staying here by yourself.'

She bit her lip again, her eyes clouding. 'I'm sorry, Nico…'

She reached out, closed her fingers around his wrist, and he thought that simple touch might be his undoing.

He forced his hand to hang by his side. 'Forget it. It's over now,' he said. And he didn't mean only the storm. He watched Marietta's face, saw the flicker of understanding in her eyes.

She withdrew her hand.

'Does it have to be?' she asked after a moment.

He stared down at her. 'I told you—'

'I know what you told me,' she interrupted. Her chin lifted. 'And I'm not suggesting any kind of commitment. I'm just suggesting that maybe…once I'm back in Rome…we could see each other occasionally.'

An uncomfortable pressure built in his chest. Had he not contemplated that very arrangement just yesterday? He suppressed a humourless laugh as an even greater irony occurred to him—having Marietta on a casual basis wouldn't be anywhere close to enough.

He hardened his voice. 'I don't do relationships—casual or otherwise.'

'Why?'

Her soft challenge poked at something inside him. Something that already felt bruised. Raw. 'Don't push, Marietta,' he warned. 'I made it clear from the outset that I couldn't offer you anything more. I thought you understood.'

She rolled forward and he stepped back.

'I understand that you're afraid, Nico,' she said softly, and stopped in front of him, meeting his gaze with another firm lift of her chin. 'I understand that you've loved and lost and now you're afraid of getting close to people, afraid of caring for anyone—because if you do you might lose them.'

Nico's blood ran cold. He felt as if she'd crawled inside him. Into the darkness he tried so hard to keep hidden.

It was shocking. Exposing.

Anger rose, swift and defensive. He paced away, turned back. 'Are you calling me a coward, Marietta?' He stalked towards her. 'That's rich, coming from you.'

Marietta's head snapped back. Nico's comeback was harsh, unexpected, landing a sharp dent in her bravado. Not that her courage had been bulletproof to start with. Mustering the nerve to seek him out and talk so frankly with him after he had avoided her all afternoon hadn't been easy.

'What do you mean?' she said.

He shook his head. 'You don't see it, do you? You're so goddamned proud, so independent—you wear it like a suit of armour so that no one can get inside it.'

She stiffened. 'I've said I'm sorry about last night—'

'I'm not just talking about last night!' He cut across her, a vein pulsing in his right temple as he stared down at her. 'You accuse *me* of being afraid—'

'It wasn't an accusation!'

'But what are *you* afraid of?' he finished.

She gripped the arms of her chair, her heart hammering wildly in her chest. 'Nothing.'

'I think that you're afraid to admit you can't do everything on your own,' he carried on, as if she hadn't spoken. 'To admit that you might actually need someone.'

Her stomach twisted. His words sliced too close to the bone. Except she wasn't afraid of needing. She was afraid of *wanting*. Or was there really no difference?

She wheeled backwards, but he followed. 'You use your independence to isolate yourself,' he said. Relentless. Ruthless. On the offensive now because she'd pushed and he had warned her not to. 'To cut yourself off from what you really want.'

She balled her hands into fists. 'You don't *know* what I want—and you're a fine one to talk about isolation. This from the man who chooses to sit up here in his house all alone and wallow in his misplaced guilt.'

Fury darkened his features. 'You know nothing about my guilt.'

'Don't I?'

A fierce ache ballooned in her chest. This exchange of harsh, angry words wasn't what she'd imagined for their last night together. She dropped her shoulders, defeat and weariness washing over her. How had they ended up here? What were they *doing*? The sudden urge to retreat tugged at her, but she loved this man—too much not to serve him a final painful truth.

'I survived a car crash that killed three of my friends,' she said. 'So I *do* know something about guilt, Nico.' She paused, took a moment to choose her next words carefully. 'What happened to Julia was tragic and horrific but it wasn't your fault—and it wasn't your father-in-law's.'

His frown deepened ominously but she forced herself to finish.

'I think it's sad that you haven't spoken to each other in ten years, and while I never knew Julia I can't believe it's what she would have wanted—nor can I believe she would have wanted you to spend the rest of your life blaming yourself for not saving her.'

Nico was tight-lipped, but the emotion she knew he tried so hard to suppress swirled in his eyes.

'You need to let go of your guilt,' she said gently. 'And if you can't do it for yourself—then do it for her.'

And for me.

She turned her chair and wheeled away from him—before the tears threatening to overwhelm her could spill.

CHAPTER TWELVE

THE NEXT MORNING they travelled in the helicopter from the island to the airstrip in Toulon, the entire journey conducted in tense, agonising silence.

Marietta's chest ached from the emotion she was bottling up inside. Tears threatened at regular intervals but she forced them back, determined to remain stoic. Even throughout the long night, as she'd lain alone in the guest bed, she'd refused to succumb, afraid that if the tears started to fall they might never stop.

When Nico carried her from the helicopter to the jet and lowered her into one of the soft leather seats she clung to him for a few seconds too long, desperate to imprint every detail of him onto her memory: his clean citrus scent, his hard male body, the bone-melting heat he exuded.

He straightened. 'Leo will collect you from the plane in Rome.'

She nodded; he had told her this morning that he wouldn't be travelling to Rome with her. Impulsively she reached for his wrist.

'Thank you,' she said. 'For…for keeping me safe.'

Flimsy, inadequate words—yet what more could she say? She couldn't tell him she loved him. Not when she knew she wouldn't hear those same words in return. And everything else—hurtful or otherwise—had been said the day before.

His gaze held hers for a long moment. Then he leaned down, cupped a hand around the side of her face and dropped a brief kiss on her mouth that brought those foolish tears springing into her eyes again.

'*Au revoir*, Marietta.'

And then he was gone.

A solitary tear escaped and she dashed it away, her insides twisting with the bitter irony of it all. Yesterday Nico had flung her fears in her face, and now he was validating them by walking away. Denying her the thing she wanted most. *Him.*

Twenty minutes later the powerful jet was soaring, and Marietta blinked as a glass half filled with amber liquid appeared on the table in front of her. She looked up. Evelyn stood by her chair, her mouth curved in a gentle smile.

'I know you like your coffee, but right now I figure you could do with something stronger.' She touched Marietta's shoulder. 'I'll give you some space, honey. Buzz if you need anything.'

Marietta murmured her thanks, then sniffed the drink and blinked at the eye-watering fumes. It was whisky rather than her favoured brandy, but she sipped it anyway, hoping the potent liquid would warm the cold, empty space inside her.

It didn't.

Nico swung the sledgehammer high above his head and smashed it down onto the centre of the beam. The wood split under the force of the blow and he finished the job off with the heel of his boot. The violent sound of splintering wood was gratifying, as was the burn in his muscles—the kind of burn only hard physical labour could induce.

It was almost a month since he'd been back here on Île de Lavande. After sending Marietta to Rome he had set himself a gruelling work schedule of back-to-back meetings and international travel, which had, for a time, kept him focused on work and nothing else. But in the end, no matter how deeply he buried himself in work, no matter how many meetings and travel destinations he piled into his schedule, he couldn't escape the simple truth.

He missed her.

'Nico!'

He looked up. Luc stood a few metres away, surrounded by the detritus of his family's boat shed. The storm had rendered the small building unsalvageable and the Bouchards had decided to knock down what remained and rebuild from scratch.

Nico had offered to help with the demolition. He

needed the distraction. Needed to escape the house he had once valued for its privacy and isolation but which now felt curiously empty and too silent.

'Break time,' said Luc, gesturing with a thumb over his shoulder towards the bistro. Josephine stood at the entrance to the courtyard, waving to catch the men's attention. Luc grinned and threw Nico a towel. 'Let's get cleaned up and grab a beer.'

Half an hour later the two men sat in the courtyard, along with Josephine's father Henri. Chilled bottles of lager sat on the wrought-iron table between them and appetising smells wafted from the kitchen. A middle-aged couple dined in the far corner of the courtyard and a small group of locals drank inside, but otherwise it was a quiet afternoon at the bistro.

Luc cradled his beer and tipped his chair back on two legs. 'How's Marietta?'

Nico's hand froze with the bottle halfway to his mouth. For appearance's sake he lifted it all the way and took a swig he hoped wouldn't choke him. 'Fine,' he said.

The younger man gave a couple of slow nods, exchanged a look with his *grandpère*, and then— to Nico's profound relief—switched the subject to football.

Ten minutes later Josephine dragged Luc away to help his father unload some supplies, leaving Nico alone with Henri.

The old man regarded him. 'You are troubled, *mon ami*.'

Nico tried to blank his expression. Henri might be long in the tooth but he was wise. Astute.

'I am fine,' he said.

Henri nodded slowly. 'So…you are fine… Marietta is fine…but things between you are *not* so fine, *oui*?'

Nico picked up his beer, realised the bottle was empty and put it down. He folded his arms over his chest.

'Things between us are…'

Over. Forgotten.

A peal of bitter laughter echoed in his head. Marietta *forgotten*? No. Far from it. She was in his mind every hour of every day, testing his resolve to forget. Only last week he'd been on the brink of flying to Rome. He'd travelled from New York to London for meetings and decided to spend the weekend at his penthouse in Paris. At the last minute he'd almost told his pilot to change the flight plan. Had entertained for a crazy moment the flawed notion that if he could have Marietta one more time, for one more night, he'd get her out of his system. His *head*.

Realising Henri was waiting for him to finish, he cast about for a suitable word and settled on, 'Complicated.'

Henri slapped his thigh and chuckled. 'Women *are* complicated, son.' He sat back, studied Nico's unsmiling face and grew serious again. 'You do not strike me as the kind of man to fear a challenge,' he said.

Nico's chest tightened. Henri's assessment of him was too generous. He feared a good many things— things Marietta had driven home to him, when she'd ruthlessly dished up a few unpalatable truths on that last night. Angry and offended, he'd accused her of labelling him a coward, but she was right. He *was* a coward. Because that night in Toulon during the storm, when he'd been out of his mind with worry, the truth of his feelings had struck with heart-stopping clarity.

He loved her—and the realisation had gripped him with unrelenting fear.

And instead of finding the strength to fight that fear he'd allowed it to control him. Had clung to his belief that loving someone again would make him weak because the fear of losing them would rule him, consume him.

But was it love that made him weak?

Or was it allowing the fear to win?

Mon Dieu. He had done exactly that. He had pushed Marietta away out of fear, to protect himself, and it wasn't only cowardly, it was selfish.

He swallowed. 'I have made a mistake, Henri.'

'Perhaps you should tell her that.'

Nico stood. *'Oui,'* he said, his thoughts clear, his mind focusing for the first time in weeks. 'But first there is someone I must see.'

* * *

The Georgian mansion nestled in the heart of the
sprawling Hudson Valley estate was unchanged from
the way Nico remembered it, its distinguished brick
façade with its shuttered windows, columned por-
tico and black front door as pristine and imposing
as ever. The lawns were still manicured, the gardens
meticulously kept, and as he walked up the white-
painted steps to the door Nico's hands felt as clammy
as they had the first time Julia had brought him here.

Before he could knock, the door opened and Barbara Lewisham stood before him.

A fist clamped tight around Nico's heart. Julia and
her mother had always looked alike, both of them
blonde and petite in size. Barbara's genteel face was
older now, and lined with the remnants of grief, but
still she reminded him of his late wife.

He braced himself, unsure of how his former
mother-in-law would receive him in person. He had
called ahead and, despite her obvious shock, she had
been civil, polite to him over the phone. But then
Barbara had always been a woman of manners and
natural reserve. Even at her daughter's funeral she'd
held her emotions in check.

She looked up at him and for a moment he thought
her grey eyes glittered with anger. Then she stepped
forward, took his hands in hers, and he realised it
was tears making her eyes shimmer.

'Nico…' she said, her smile tremulous. 'It is so good to see you.'

The genuine warmth she conveyed threw him. He'd expected coolness from her at best. Hostility at worst. They hadn't spoken much in the days leading up to Julia's funeral, or afterwards. He'd assumed that she shared her husband's view of things. Had he been wrong?

'And you, Barbara,' he said.

She led him into the grand foyer and closed the door. 'Jack's in the study.'

'You told him I was coming?'

'He's expecting you.' She gestured towards the wood-panelled hallway that Nico remembered led to Jack Lewisham's study. 'Go ahead.'

The door was closed when he got there—which was not, he thought, a particularly welcoming sign. He took a deep, even breath, knocked once and entered.

'Hello, Jack.'

Jack Lewisham turned from the window where he stood across the room, and Nico kept his expression impassive as he registered the physical changes time had wrought in the man. He was still tall—six foot— and broad-shouldered, but the deep lines scoring his face and the grey streaking his hair made him look as if he'd aged twenty years rather than ten.

He didn't stride forward to shake Nico's hand. Instead he nodded a silent greeting, walked across the Persian rug to an antique sideboard and poured whisky from a crystal decanter into two cut-glass tumblers.

He took the glasses to a small table set between two deep leather chairs, and finally spoke. 'Will you join me?'

The invitation was stiff, the words wooden, and yet more polite than Nico had expected. Wary, his palms still clammy, he crossed the room and sat down.

Jack sipped his whisky. 'I see your company is doing well.'

Nico picked up his glass, inclined his head. 'It is.' He paused, then added, 'I'm not here to talk about my company, Jack.'

The older man eyed him for a long moment. He took a larger slug of whisky. 'I tried to talk her out of marrying you, you know.'

'I'm aware,' Nico said flatly.

'As a kid, she always had a thing for strays.'

Nico slammed his glass onto the table and stood. *Dieu*. What insanity had brought him here? He turned and started towards the door.

'Nico.'

Jack's voice halted him. He turned back. The man was on his feet, his mouth set in a grim line.

'I apologise,' Jack said hoarsely. 'It wasn't what I meant to say. Please…' He ran his hand through his hair. 'Stay.'

Nico hesitated, tension vibrating in every muscle, his gut churning with anger and indecision. After a moment he walked back, sat again.

'Thank you,' Jack said, lowering himself to the edge of his chair. He rested his elbows on his knees, scrubbed a hand over his face before speaking again. 'Julia had a good heart, is what I was trying to say. And she was smart—an excellent judge of character.' He paused, looked Nico in the eye. 'Despite my reservations in the beginning it didn't take me long to realise she'd chosen a good man.'

Emotion punched through Nico's chest, so swift and powerful his lungs were left airless for a moment.

'Losing her was the worst thing that had ever happened to me,' Jack went on. 'I didn't know how to handle it. The anger, the grief…' He bowed his head. 'I blamed you, but it was my fault…*my* fault,' he repeated, his voice bleak, filled with self-loathing. 'I was arrogant, stupid—'

He broke off, his body heaving with a sob that seemed torn from him, and Nico instinctively reached over, gripped the man's shoulder.

'You tried to save her,' he said. 'We both did—and we failed. But we are not to blame for her death. That responsibility lies with the men who took her.'

And for the first time in ten years, he truly believed that.

Jack looked up, his eyes deeply shadowed, his

face ravaged by years of grief and self-recrimination. 'I don't know how to move beyond it.'

Nico firmed his grip on Jack's shoulder. 'You have to let go of the guilt,' he said, his throat thickening as Marietta's voice echoed in his head.

Jack nodded and they sat in silence for a moment. And then they talked—until the whisky decanter was nearly empty and the shadows outside had lengthened across the manicured lawns.

Barbara ventured in to ask Nico if he would stay for supper. He accepted, and then excused himself to place a call.

Though it was already evening, his assistant at his New York office answered on the first ring.

'I need to travel on the jet out of LaGuardia first thing tomorrow,' he said.

'Yes, sir. Destination?'

'Rome.'

Marietta stared at the printout of the ultrasound image and felt all the same emotions she'd experienced the *first* time Helena and Leo had announced they were expecting: joy, excitement, happiness, and envy.

That last one she tried not to feel too keenly.

'Oh, Helena!' She leaned forward in her chair and threw her arms around her sister-in-law. 'I'm so happy for you. A little sister or brother for Riccardo.'

Helena hugged her back. 'I know—I'm so excited.'

Marietta was thrilled for her brother and his wife. They deserved every happiness. Their road to love had been rocky, and eight years ago their first child—an unplanned baby—had been stillborn. The tragedy had affected both of them deeply, even though Leo hadn't learnt about his son until some years after the event.

Ridiculously, her eyes began to prickle.

Helena looked at her. 'Marietta—what's wrong?'

'Nothing. I'm happy for you, that's all.'

She blinked the tears back and forced a smile. She'd left Île de Lavande over a month ago and still she was an emotional wreck. She needed to pull herself together, get back to being her old self, and yet she'd started to suspect with an awful sinking sensation in her stomach that her 'old self' was long gone and wasn't ever coming back.

Because her 'old self' would have celebrated the lucrative commission she'd recently landed with a night out with friends, instead of sitting at home alone with a glass of brandy and the DVD of a silly romantic movie—and, worse, *crying* over that movie.

Her 'old self' would have gone about her day with her usual vigour and would *not* have felt her heart surge every time she saw a tall dark-haired man, only to feel it shrink again when she realised it wasn't him.

Her 'old self' would have noticed the black vehicles with their tinted windows and the occasional watchful man in the shadows and felt outraged, instead of feeling her heart swell with the knowledge that he was still protecting her, from a distance.

And her 'old self' definitely *wouldn't* be sitting here feeling envious of her sister-in-law, wishing she had a handsome husband and children of her own to shower with love and affection.

Helena was still looking at her and she slipped her sunglasses on. They were sitting in the landscaped garden at Leo and Helena's Tuscan villa, enjoying the late morning sun and some 'girl time' while Leo entertained Ricci indoors. Autumn had arrived but the days were still warm, and the air carried the fragrance of flowers and fruits from the neighbouring orchards. Marietta had travelled up for the weekend, hoping a change of scenery would lift her mood.

'How far along are you?' she asked.

'Ten weeks.' Helena frowned. 'You know, you haven't seemed like yourself since you came back from the island.'

Marietta tried to keep her smile intact but the very worst thing happened—her lips quivered.

'Oh, Marietta.' Helena reached for her hand. 'What is it? Tell me.'

'I slept with Nico,' she blurted out, because she simply couldn't keep it secret any longer. She needed to talk about it with someone or she'd lose her mind. She stared at her sister-in-law, waiting for the look of shock. Of censure.

'Well,' said Helena, 'I can't say I'm surprised.'

Marietta's jaw slackened. 'You're not?'

'No. I'm not.' She let go of Marietta's hand and refilled their glasses from a pitcher of homemade lemonade on the table. 'I saw the way he looked at you on my wedding day, Marietta.' She picked up her glass, sat back and smiled. 'He couldn't take his eyes off you.'

Marietta frowned. She remembered Nico from the wedding day. He'd been impossible to miss. Aside from her brother he'd been the tallest man there, and by far the most eye-catching in his tux. But she'd taken one dry-mouthed look at his powerful body and his chiselled features, reminded herself that men like him were out of her league, and then steadfastly kept her gaze off him.

'I take it things didn't end well?' Helena said gently.

Marietta shook her head. 'I ended up wanting more than he could give.'

Helena exhaled on a sigh. 'Don't tell me he's one of those men who's allergic to commitment.'

'He's a widower,' she said, and this time her sister-in-law's face *did* register shock.

'I had no idea.'

'Leo doesn't know?'

'If he does he's never said anything. I'm guessing Nico has some issues, then?'

'A few.'

She wanted to share more with Helena, but Nico was an intensely private man and talking about his past—particularly the gruesome story of his wife's death—felt wrong. And then Leo appeared, carrying Ricci in his arms, and the little boy gurgled and squealed when he saw his mother.

Helena stood to take him, and he squealed again when she blew a raspberry kiss on his plump rosy cheek.

Leo put his hand to his wife's back, said something in her ear. Helena looked at Marietta and frowned. Her mouth opened, but Leo cut her off with a few quietly spoken words and then urged her indoors. Helena resisted, gave her husband a stern look and walked back to Marietta.

'I'll be right inside if you need me,' she said, squeezing Marietta's shoulder, and then she took Ricci into the house.

Confused, Marietta looked to her brother.

'Nico's here,' he said without preamble. 'He wants to see you.'

Her brain stalled. Nico was *here?* She blinked, trying to process the fact. 'How did he know where I was?'

'He called me and I told him.'

'Why didn't you say anything?'

'Because he asked me not to. And, frankly, he sounded…desperate.' Leo scowled. 'Do you want to tell me what the hell is going on, Marietta?'

She pulled in a deep breath, her heart pounding. 'Not particularly.'

A muscle flexed in her brother's jaw.

'Do you wish to see him?'

She hesitated. Briefly. *'Si,'* she said, and instantly her stomach quivered.

Leo strode into the house and a minute later Nico emerged. He walked towards her, smart and handsome in black trousers and a grey button-down shirt, his strong jaw clean-shaven, his dark hair cropped short. Her heart somersaulted. How could he look so good, so *unchanged*, when she felt so fundamentally altered? It wasn't fair.

'Bonjour, Marietta.'

His deep voice washed over her and just like that, with a few velvety syllables, all the heartache of the last month was swept away by a surge of heat and longing she was helpless to prevent.

'Buongiorno, Nico,' she managed, her voice cool. Composed. Silently she congratulated herself. No need for him to see how he affected her.

He gestured to the seat Helena had vacated. 'May I?'

She nodded, and he moved the chair closer to her before he sat. His proximity made her skin tingle. Her pulse race.

'I've missed you.'

Her insides clenched on another surge of longing. *I've missed you too*, she wanted to say.

'Did you come all the way to Tuscany to tell me you missed me, Nico?'

The corners of his mouth tilted, as though he were amused, and she wished he wouldn't smile. It weakened her.

'I did,' he said simply.

And that made her eyes sting, because she wanted so very badly to believe him.

Suddenly he moved, reaching towards her, and before she could stop him he'd pulled her sunglasses off her face.

His gaze narrowed. 'You don't believe me, *ma petite sirène?*'

'Please don't call me that.'

'Why not?'

Did he really need to ask?

'Nico, please…just tell me why you're here.'

He hesitated. 'I'd like to take you somewhere.'

'Where?'

'It's a surprise.'

Her stomach fluttered. 'I don't like surprises.'

'Please,' he said, and she heard the distinct note of uncertainty, of vulnerability, in his voice.

It weakened her.

Still, she made him wait a few seconds more. 'Okay,' she said at last, and his features relaxed a fraction.

He stood. 'Do you trust me, *chérie?*'

She nodded, because she did. She had always

trusted him and she always would. All the same, she wasn't expecting him to do what he did next—which was to lean down and scoop her out of her chair.

'Nico!' she exclaimed.

He carried her through the garden and round the side of the villa to the courtyard out front. A large black vehicle was waiting, a man dressed in black standing beside it. He opened the rear passenger door and Nico slid her into the back seat, closed the door, and a few seconds later climbed in beside her from the opposite side. He rapped on the dark glass partition that separated them from the driver and the vehicle started to move.

Nico reached across her—to strap the seatbelt over her, she assumed. But he hauled her into his lap.

'Nico—'

He kissed her, and shamefully, wantonly, she made no effort to resist. Instead she surrendered, snaking her arms around his neck and kissing him back.

It was a hot, hungry meeting of lips, and when they finally broke apart he was breathing hard. His large hands cradled her face, his blue eyes heated and glittering. '*Mon Dieu*, I missed you.'

Marietta trembled. 'Nico,' she pleaded. 'Tell me what's going on.'

He pressed his forehead to hers, the gesture so sweet that her chest flooded with tenderness and something else. Something she was too afraid to acknowledge.

'I don't know where to start,' he said.

'Start at the beginning,' she said softly.

He nodded, and took a deep breath. 'The morning after the storm, when I got back to the house and found the shattered window and you nowhere in sight, it was like Julia all over again—arriving home, finding her gone... I couldn't breathe... couldn't think...'

Marietta's throat ached. She laid her hand along the side of his face. 'I'm so sorry for putting you through that,' she whispered.

He placed his hand over hers, turned his head and kissed her palm, then tucked her hand against his chest and held it there.

'Losing her inflicted wounds I thought would never heal, and I was determined to never feel that pain again. To never feel that sense of loss and devastation.'

He fell silent. Marietta waited.

'You were right, *chérie*. I was afraid. Afraid to care for someone. Afraid to love again. But then...' He gave her a crooked smile. 'You came along.'

A jolt of warmth, of hope, went through her.

'And you were right about something else,' he said. 'I needed to deal with my guilt—confront the past.' He paused. 'I went to see Jack.'

Her eyes widened. 'And...?'

He grimaced. 'It wasn't easy, but we talked. Laid some demons to rest.'

'Oh, Nico… I'm so proud of you.'

'Don't be.' His mouth flattened. 'I pushed you away, and that's nothing to be proud of. I told myself it was the logical thing to do but it was logic driven by fear—a weak man's excuse.'

She frowned. 'You're *not* weak,' she declared. 'And you're not the only one who's been driven by fear.'

Nico shook his head. 'I shouldn't have said—'

She pressed her fingers to his lips. 'But you were right. I isolated myself, just like you did—but in a different way and for different reasons. I was afraid, too. Afraid of wanting what I couldn't have.'

Nico took hold of her slender fingers and kissed their tips one by one. He loved this woman. When he'd walked down that garden path and caught his first glimpse of her—beautiful in a simple white top and long skirt, her glorious hair flowing loose over her shoulders—he'd thought his chest might implode.

'And what *do* you want, *ma belle?*'

'You,' she said, a fierce light shining in her eyes.

He cupped her face in his hands. 'Marietta Vincenti, will you do me the honour of letting me love you?'

Tears welled in her eyes. She placed her hands over his. 'If you'll do me the honour of letting *me* love *you*.'

The car stopped and he kissed her, briefly, but with enough intensity to let her know there'd be more to come.

'I love you,' he said.

Then he lowered the window and pointed towards the middle of the large meadow by which they'd stopped. She blinked, and her eyes widened as she saw a fully inflated, brightly coloured hot air balloon.

'Will you come fly with me, *chérie*?'

Her mouth stretched into a grin. 'I thought you said hot air balloons are dangerous.'

He'd also said it would be a frosty day in hell when he flew in one. Well…today hell was having a cold snap.

A short while later the 'oversized picnic basket'—as Nico was fond of calling it—lifted off the ground. Marietta felt like a child. Breathless, giddy, excited. Or maybe like a woman in love. She sat on a special stool, high enough to enjoy the stunning view of the Tuscan countryside, with Nico's arms circling her from behind, his chest solid and warm against her back.

She jumped at the sudden loud whoosh as the pilot fired the burner, and Nico's hold tightened.

'I've got you, *chérie*.'

She smiled up at him. 'I know. I've got you, too.'

For ever.

EPILOGUE

'Papà! Papà!'

A flash of pink and lime-green hurtled through the doorway of the study.

Nico swivelled his chair around. 'Amélie, don't run in the—*oomph!*'

His six-year-old daughter catapulted herself into his lap, and the moment she grinned up at him he forgot to finish scolding her. He closed his arms around her wriggling body and grinned back.

Amélie was a brown-eyed, dark-haired mini-version of her mother, and too damned adorable to stay cross with for very long—even when she pushed his patience to its limits. Which she did—frequently—because she'd inherited not only Marietta's beauty but a good deal of her stubbornness as well.

'Can we go to the beach now, Papa?'

And, like her mother, she loved to swim in the sea.

'In a bit, *ma petite sirène*.'

Her little lips formed a pout that was no doubt designed to weaken her *papà*. 'But I want to go *now*. Enzo's already there, with Remy. Why can't I go down the steps by myself like they can?'

'Because they are older and bigger.'

The tiny scowl on her face looked a lot like the one her mother occasionally wore when Nico earned her disapproval. Fortunately for him, those occasions were rare—and he always enjoyed it when they made up afterwards.

He scooted his daughter off his lap. 'Go and help *Maman* prepare the picnic hamper.'

He watched his daughter fly out of the room. Her energy was boundless, and these days it seemed she was incapable of *walking* anywhere. Enzo, his ten-year-old son, had gone through a similar stage, which had included climbing anything in sight that looked remotely scaleable.

Nico had been convinced he was destined for heart failure—especially in those first few years of parenting. On the day his son had been born he'd known fierce pride and elation, but also a sort of quiet terror. A fear that he would somehow fail to protect this tiny life in a world increasingly fraught with danger and risk.

Marietta had known. Whether she'd seen something in his face or simply sensed his inner turmoil, she had understood. And she had talked him down. Helped him to wrestle his fear into something less daunting, more controllable. And as their son had grown, she had insisted they did not wrap him in cotton wool. Had insisted that their son be allowed to experience the world. To grow up as safely as possible, yet with an understanding of risk and consequence.

It was Marietta, too, who had convinced him they should have a second child. Nico had been hesitant after her first pregnancy. Blood pressure problems and other issues related to her paralysis had dogged her from the second trimester onwards. He had watched her struggle with long months of enforced bed rest and vowed he wouldn't see her suffer like that again.

But she was resilient, and strong, and she'd set her heart on a little sister or brother for Enzo. And his wife had, of course, proved very persuasive in bed...

Nico closed his laptop. He had cleared enough emails and reports for today. Marietta growled if he spent too much time working during their family vacations on Île de Lavande.

He stood and his gaze caught, as it sometimes did, on the antique rolltop desk in the corner of the study.

Julia's ghost had been laid to rest many years before. Very occasionally the darkness and the guilt would stir in some deep corner of his soul, but the emotions never lasted for long—not in the face of the light and the laughter that his children and his wife brought to his world. He'd considered at one point getting rid of the desk, but Marietta had convinced him not to and he was glad she had.

He found his girls in the kitchen. Amélie launched herself into his arms again and he lifted her up.

'Now, Papa? Can we go *now?*'

He looked to Marietta and felt the familiar jolt in his blood. Her hair, still long and lustrous, was pulled into a ponytail and she wore a sarong and a crimson bikini top, ready for the beach. Into her forties now, she was as beautiful as ever—and she still made his body hum with desire.

'Are you finished with your little helper?'

She wheeled back from one of the low marble benches they'd had specially installed for her and smiled. '*Si*. And the hamper's ready. Take Amélie and the basket down—and don't forget to come back for your wife.'

He slid a hand around the back of her head and dropped a quick kiss on her teasing mouth. 'Funny, Mrs César.'

She grinned and his heart expanded—and he wondered, not for the first time over the years, how his chest could feel so full and yet so incredibly, amazingly light.

Marietta lay on a towel on the sand with her eyes closed, enjoying the sun on her face and the sound of her husband and children playing in the ocean. Nico had already taken her in for a swim and she was content now to relax and let the kids frolic under his watchful eye.

This was her reality now. The one that in the early years of her marriage she had secretly feared wasn't reality at all, but a fantastical dream of some sort. A great big bubble of joy that would sooner or later burst and send her crashing back to her *real* life.

But the bubble hadn't burst. It had only grown bigger and stronger—like her love for her husband—and eventually she'd stopped waiting on tenterhooks for the fairy tale to end and allowed herself to truly enjoy the life she'd never thought she'd have.

She smiled at the sound of Amélie's high-pitched squeal and guessed her *papà* was throwing her into the air. She could hear the boys too. Her son and Remy Bouchard—Luc's son—were firm friends, and Remy usually stayed with them for a few nights when they vacationed here.

She could not believe she and Nico had been married for almost thirteen years. They had finally settled in Paris, and they lived there in a beautiful home they'd renovated and fully modified for her wheelchair. They'd sold her apartment in Rome, but retained Nico's apartments in London, New York and Singapore, all of which he used when travelling for work.

Marietta happily divided her time between motherhood and her art career, which had flourished in the early years of their marriage and continued to keep her busy now, with several lucrative commissions each year.

She heard Nico's deep voice telling Enzo to watch his sister and then her son's obedient response. She smiled again. Enzo was becoming more like his father every day—serious and intense—but he also had a strong streak of curiosity about the world which showed he had something of his mother in him.

'What are you smiling about, *chérie*?'

She looked up through her sunglasses at her husband and her stomach clenched, because he was still the most magnificent man she knew. Dripping wet, he stretched out on a towel beside her and she marvelled at how hard and toned his body had remained over the years. Physically, he really hadn't changed. A few distinguished-looking grey hairs at his temples and some deeper lines on his face due to his secretly worrying about his wife and children, but otherwise he looked the same.

And he still loved her—as fiercely and passionately as he had in the beginning.

'I was just thinking,' she said, tracing her index finger along the strong line of his jaw, 'that Enzo is very much like his *papà*.'

Nico grinned—and she melted. She always did when her husband smiled at her.

His chest puffed out. 'But of course. He is good-looking, intelligent, irresistible—'

She slapped her hand over his mouth. 'And lacking in modesty!'

Her took her hand and pressed a kiss into her palm. 'And our daughter is very much like her *maman*.'

'*Si*. Beautiful, talented—'

'Stubborn, wilful—and her wish list is already longer than her mother's was!'

She laughed. 'A girl needs to dream.'

And yet her own wish list was practically non-existent now, because she had everything she could possibly want—and more.

All the things that had originally been on her list had been ticked off early in their marriage, before they'd started trying for children. Nico had taken her to Egypt to see the pyramids and the Valley of the Kings, and the trip had been magical—despite a team of his security men shadowing them everywhere they went. They'd gone up in a hot air balloon again—on their honeymoon—and eventually, after much persistence on her part, he'd agreed to her doing a tandem skydive. But not before he'd vetted the skydiving company and warned the operator that if anything happened to his wife he would personally throw the man out of a plane *without* his parachute.

The only things she wished for now were health and happiness for her family.

She looked at Nico, propped on his elbow, staring down at her. 'And why are *you* smiling, *tesoro mio*?'

He trailed a fingertip over her bare belly, inciting a flurry of goosebumps on her skin. 'Because I've arranged for Luc to collect the children in an hour's time and take them to his place for the night.'

A hot spark of anticipation ignited in her belly. She arched an eyebrow. 'And what will you do then?'

'Then, *ma belle*,' he said, his blue eyes smouldering, 'I will spend the night showing my wife how much I love her.'

* * * * *

Don't forget to read the first part of
Angela Bissell's
IRRESISTIBLE MEDITERRANEAN
TYCOONS *duet*
SURRENDERING TO THE VENGEFUL ITALIAN
Available now!

#3501 BRIDE BY ROYAL DECREE
Wedlocked!
by Caitlin Crews

King Reza's betrothed, Princess Magdalena, disappeared years ago. But a mysterious photograph brings them together again. Fiercely independent Maggy won't accept her birthright on any terms but her own—so Reza will have to use sensual persuasions that Maggy will be helpless to resist!

#3502 THE SHEIKH'S SECRET SON
Secret Heirs of Billionaires
by Maggie Cox

Sheikh Zafir el-Kalil will do anything to secure his child—even marry the woman who kept their son a secret! But Darcy Carrick is older and wiser now, and it will take more than soft words and sweet seduction to win back her love...

#3503 ACQUIRED BY HER GREEK BOSS
by Chantelle Shaw

Greek tycoon Alekos Gionakis thinks he knows his secretary, until he's forced to reappraise his most precious asset! Alekos offers beautiful Sara Lovejoy a meeting with her unknown family, provided she agrees to become his mistress. But Sara's innocence is priceless...

#3504 VOWS THEY CAN'T ESCAPE
by Heidi Rice

Xanthe Carmichael has discovered two things: that she's *still* married, and her husband could take half her business! Xanthe is hit by lust when she confronts him with divorce papers...but will Dane begin stirring the smoldering embers of their passion?

HARLEQUIN *Presents*®

**Don't miss Heidi Rice's thrilling
Harlequin Presents debut—a story of
a couple tempestuously reunited!**

Xanthe Carmichael has just discovered two things:
1. Her ex-husband could take half her business
2. She's actually still married to him!

When she jets off to New York, divorce papers in hand, Xanthe
is prepared for the billionaire bad boy's slick offices…but not for
the spear of lust that hits her the moment she sees Dane Redmond
again! Has her body no shame, no recollection of the pain he
caused? But Dane is stalling… Is he really checking the fine print
or planning to stir the smoldering embers of their passion and
tempt her back into the marriage bed?

Don't miss

*VOWS THEY
CAN'T ESCAPE*

Available February 2017

HP06044

Alessandro was so different than she was. Gabby had never truly fully appreciated just how different men and women were. In a million ways, big and small.

Yes, there was the obvious, but it was more than that. And it was those differences that suddenly caused her to glory in who she was, what she was. To feel, if only for a moment, that she completely understood herself both body and soul, and that they were united in one desire.

"Kiss me, Princess," he said, his voice low, strained.

He was affected.

So she had won.

She had been the one to make him burn.

But she'd made a mistake if she'd thought this game had one winner and one loser. She was right down there with him. And she didn't care about winning anymore.

She couldn't deny him, not now. Not when he was

looking at her like she was a woman and not a girl, or an owl. Not when he was looking at her like she was the sun, moon and all the stars combined. Bright, brilliant and something that held the power to hold him transfixed.

Something more than what she was. Because Gabriella D'Oro had never transfixed anyone. Not her parents. Not a man.

But he was looking at her like she mattered. She didn't feel like shrinking into a wall or melting into the scenery. She wanted him to keep looking.

She didn't want to hide from this. She wanted all of it.

Slowly, so slowly, so that she could savor the feel of him, relish the sensations of his body beneath her touch, she slid her hand up his throat, feeling the heat of his skin, the faint scratch of whiskers.

Then she moved to cup his jaw, his cheek.

"I've never touched a man like this before," she confessed.

And she wasn't even embarrassed by the confession, because he was still looking at her like he wanted her.

He moved closer, covering her hand with his. She could feel his heart pounding heavily, could sense the tension running through his frame. "I've touched a great many women," he said, his tone grave. "But at the moment it doesn't seem to matter."

That was when she kissed him.

Don't miss
THE LAST DI SIONE CLAIMS HIS PRIZE,
available February 2017 wherever
Harlequin Presents® books and ebooks are sold.

www.Harlequin.com